DESERT AMBUSH

Keeshah's head and neckfur lifted simultaneously and he called the warning: *Danger.*

He whirled to face north, his head high and questing for the source of what he scented. Tarani hadn't heard Keeshah's mental warning, but she couldn't mistake his reaction. She was on her feet immediately, the steel sword in her hand.

I had my sword ready, too, and was running to join Keeshah and Tarani when vineh seemed to boil up out of the sand.

I counted fifteen before I got too busy to worry about it.

D0348641

THE GANDALARA CYCLE

VI
RETURN TO EDDARTA

RANDALL GARRETT and VICKI ANN HEYDRON

BANTAM BOOKS

TORONTO • NEW YORK • LONDON • SYDNEY • AUCKLAND

RETURN TO EDDARTA
A Bantam Book / March 1985

Map by Robert J. Sabuda

ISBN 0-553-24709-3

Published simultaneously in the United States and Canada

Bantam Books are published by Bantam Books, Inc. Its trademark,
consisting of the words "Bantam Books" and the portrayal of a
rooster, is Registered in U.S. Patent and Trademark Office and in
other countries. Marca Registrada. Bantam Books, Inc., 666 Fifth
Avenue, New York, New York 10103.

PRINTED IN THE UNITED STATES OF AMERICA

O   0 9 8 7 6 5 4 3 2 1

RETURN TO EDDARTA

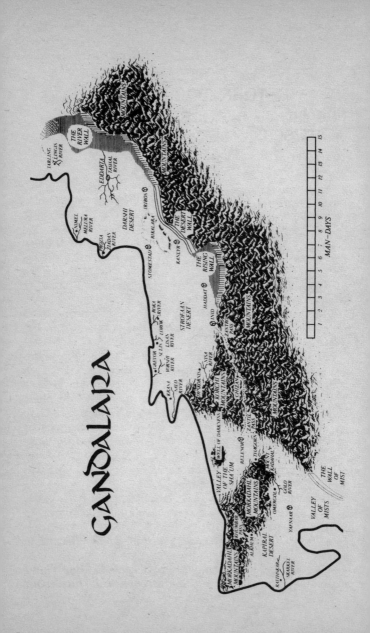

PRELIMINARY PROCEEDINGS: INPUT SESSION SIX

—Recorder?

—Yes, I am here. The Record has been too long neglected, I think.

—I agree, of course. Give me a few minutes to prepare for my absence, and I will join you presently.

—I am embarrassed, Recorder, that you were forced to seek me out to complete the Record.

—My action is a small matter. Of more consequence is the cause of it. You have been too deeply involved in the details of the task you have set yourself.

—I thought Recorders refrained from value judgments.

—Do not smile away the issue, I beg you. You know very well that the abstinence of judgment applies particularly to the content of the Record; I am but a channel for your thoughts and memories as they enter the All-Mind. Outside my role as Recorder, I am as likely to praise or criticize as anyone. And anyone can see that you have had too little rest in recent weeks.

—Surely you don't mean to say that continuing the Record will be restful for me?

—Hardly. The trance state in which your body exists while the Record is being made cannot be compared to natural sleep.

—Then you expect this next portion of the Record to soothe me?

—Again I ask you to take this matter less lightly. What I expect is that continuing the Record will turn your *attention from detail to purpose, and encourage you to care for yourself.*

—Oh.

—Forgive me. I did not know that my concern would express itself as anger.

—The rebuke is well deserved, Recorder. As Ricardo might say, I've been fiddling with the trees and forgetting the forest. And you're absolutely right; the Record is a potent reminder of the forest. I'm ready when you are.

—My anger disturbed the serenity I require to Record. I will need a moment to compose myself.

—I need that moment as well. It has been so long since our last session that I'm not sure where to begin this one. . . . Yes, of course.

Tarani and I had ridden my sha'um, Keeshah, into the Kapiral desert. We had found Kä, the abandoned capital of the ancient kingdom, and the sword still hidden there. We were returning to Raithskar and Keeshah's family—Yayshah and the three newborn cubs.

—I am calm now. Are you ready to continue?

—I am ready, Recorder.

—Then make your mind one with mine, as I have made mine one with the All-Mind. . . .

—WE BEGIN!

2

1

Kä vanished back into the desert with a speed and completeness that amazed me. The ancient city stood in the open air, the stonework of the oldest part of the city little harmed by the passing centuries. Closer to the city's perimeter, the streets were still recognizable as level pathways threading through thousands of shapeless mounds. Each mound represented the remains of a building constructed of salt blocks, a sensible building material for the extensive desert areas in Gandalara.

Even the desert air had to have some tiny percentage of moisture, however indetectable by warm skin seeking relief from the heat. That moisture, combined with the weight of the upper portions of the buildings, had broken down the crystalline structure of the lower blocks; the inexorable process, and the hardly noticeable movement of air, had rounded and smoothed the top layers.

Stop for a second, I thought to Keeshah.

Just started, his mindvoice grumbled, but he slowed down.

I had been stretched out, clinging to the big cat's back with elbow and knee pressure. Tarani was riding second, seated close to the cat's hips with her lithe body pressed over mine. We sat up as Keeshah slowed—the coolness that swept against my back when Tarani removed her warmth always filled me with a sense of loss—and turned to look back at the apparently empty desert.

"It still amazes me that Kä has never been rediscovered,"

Tarani said. "It is hidden only to those who do not try to find it."

"So it is safely hidden," I said, "for no one else has tried—probably, since Zanek shared Serkajon's body as a Visitor, and returned to Kä to hide the King's sword."

From the corner of my eye, I saw her hand move to the hilt of the steel sword, which had replaced its bronze cousin in her baldric. The bronze sword hung beside it, its hilt caught by the baldric and the flat of the blade braced against the thigh and calf of her bent leg.

"It remains a mystery to me," Tarani said, shaking her head. "So great a city—would no one have been curious about it?"

"That's the Recorder in you talking," I told her. "You've been trained to respect the value of the past, and to learn about it as fact, without emotional involvement. Kä was left behind a long time ago. The people on this side of the Morkadahls have an oral history strongly colored by Serkajon's heroic image and the presence of the Sharith. No one west of Relenor has *wanted* to find it."

"I see that," she admitted thoughtfully. "Yet the Kingdom is well remembered and still respected—however mistakenly—by the Lords of Eddarta. Why have they not begun a search?"

"We don't know that they haven't," I reminded her. "But again, I strongly doubt it. Think of the distance between here and Eddarta, and the difficulty of the two high crossings near Chizan. And remember that *we* have the advantage of a sha'um. They would be on foot, unfamiliar with the landmarks west of the Morkadahls, attempting a desert search after the long haul from Eddarta."

"It does seem unlikely that the Lords would willingly undergo so much privation for curiosity's sake," Tarani said. "So—those who could have found Kä have not cared to, and those who might have cared to, could not." She looked in the direction of Kä again. "I cannot wish it forgotten, Rikardon. At its end, it was an evil place. Yet the spirit that founded it was noble, and its purpose well served for many generations."

Go now? Keeshah asked, shifting his weight restlessly.

"Keeshah is eager to move on," I said.

4

"I expect he is looking forward to being with his family again," Tarani said. "Yayshah awaits him eagerly. It is time for us to abandon Kä one final time."

We settled ourselves again into riding position. Tarani needed an extra moment to adjust the positions of the swords, then Keeshah set off at a run northwesterly, toward Raithskar.

Carrying both those swords must be awkward for Tarani, I thought. *Yet I wouldn't think of leaving the bronze sword behind, or even offer to carry it for her. Both swords are hers—and her responsibility.*

Pressing my face into Keeshah's fur, I slipped into the familiar state of reverie in which non-Gandalaran Ricardo, an objective (more or less) observer, analyzed native Markasset's actions and attitudes. A blending of human mind and Gandalaran memory was occasionally (not always) an advantage. I frequently had been confounded by the fact that Markasset didn't know everything I wanted to know about this world.

I realized that I had found the answer to more than one mystery in the All-Mind. When Somil had guided me to Zanek's lifememory and allowed me to share it, for those few brief moments, I had been exposed to all of Zanek's knowledge, to his society, and to its immediate past history—all of which lay hundreds of generations in the past, from Markasset's perspective. And swords were very much a feature of Zanek's world.

During my first hour or so in this world, weak and disoriented, I had forced myself to take the sword of a dead man and drag it across the desert—until I no longer had the strength to move it. Later, the—call it a talisman—that had sparked the integration of Markasset's memories with Ricardo's personality had been a very special sword. With Markasset's training, the steel sword called Rika had saved my life with unsettling frequency. More than that, its presence had often provided me with an odd sense of comfort.

Surely, the feeling I had for Rika was partly a sense of security in having a superior weapon. The blade carried a memory of that moment of integration, and of the emotion-packed realization that Markasset's father thought me more

5

worthy than his own son to carry the treasured sword. But there was another feeling, deeper than any of these. The closest thing to it in Ricardo's experience was the feeling he often had when watching a fire burn in a fireplace. Far away in time and culture and thought patterns from the crouching near-men who had first discovered the benefits of fire, he had been subject still to an atavistic thrill of *power*—the power to survive.

Up until now, the Ricardo part of me had marked the significance of personal weapons as a remnant of barbaric tradition in the highly cultured Gandalaran society. The sword is designed for fighting, not hunting, and is more connected with aggression than survival. It cannot be thrown as easily as a spear, and it does not have the close-quarters maneuverability of a small, sharp knife. I had been assuming that the Gandalaran sword had developed out of the inter-city warfare that had so appalled Zanek.

Nope.

In Gandalara, the sword *was* developed as a survival weapon—for survival against vineh. The apelike beasts were a branch from the same family tree as Gandalaran people. They walked on two legs, lived in colony groups, and carried impressive natural weapons: huge grasping hands with nails tough as claws, mouths built to open wide and clamp hard, and a whole lot of muscle. Vineh were omnivores. They had many of the same environmental needs as Gandalarans, and were inclined to be ungenerous about sharing territory.

Both the vineh and the Gandalarans would have been nomadic hunter-gatherers in the beginning; territorial conflict might have been frequent. Adult male vineh were bigger and stronger than the men of Gandalara, but the men would have had the advantages of intelligence and greater group cooperation. That probably meant, at first, that the men knew when to run, and maintained an orderly retreat—preventing useless losses.

Once the Gandalarans had discovered cultivation, and the need to stay in one place for more than a season, whatever leisure their expanding and specializing culture could offer would have been directed toward more efficient defense: a sharpened stone; tied to the end of a stick to compensate for the vineh's longer reach; tied along the edge of a stick for close-quarters fighting; pieces of hammered metal in place of the stones to make the weapon a bit lighter; a strip of hammered metal; metal alloys that kept an edge longer; the idea to sharpen both edges and the search for an alloy that could be used without a center rod of breakable wood.

The people of Gandalara had one other major advantage over the vineh: the All-Mind. The shared memory would have made technological advances available to everyone, and would have allowed new generations to benefit from the learning of the past ones, without the need to rely on oral history or wait for writing to be developed. Settlements would have grown quickly, forcing the vineh to find other, perhaps less desirable territory that offered natural shelter.

By Zanek's time, all the vineh west of the Morkadahls had moved into the rocky, almost desert terrain in the hills just west of Raithskar, and continued to be a major nuisance. Some visionary before Zanek had designed Raithskar, with its center and radiant squares, and had guided the building of the impressive stone wall that had since been copied by other cities. In Zanek's time, the Sharith had been part of city government and patrolled the perimeter of cultivated land, to keep people in the fields safe from vineh. I found myself wishing Zanek had known the identity of the first man who had brought a sha'um across the Alkhum Pass to share his life in Raithskar; I wanted to thank him.

But even by Zanek's time, the All-Mind had become an accessible but indirect source of information, and the knowledge contained in it (Rikardon might speak of it analogously as a data base) had grown too large for comprehension by any single individual. I suspected it had been too large almost at once, but that the connection between individuals and All-Mind had been stronger when the survival of the race had depended on the ability of one to share the knowledge of the others.

The All-Mind still played a part in Gandalaran life. I felt sure that the "inner awareness" available to every person was an extension of the common experience in the All-Mind. But conscious contact with the phenomenon was

7

limited to those with the proper training, called Recorders. I had worked with two very recently: Somil in Omergol, the capable, quite colorful, "rogue" Recorder who had introduced me to Zanek and found the general location of Kä for me; and the woman whose weight rested pleasantly against my back.

Almost as if she had felt me thinking about her, she stirred. Her hands tightened on my shoulders as she braced her legs higher on Keeshah's hips. Hands and legs remained tensed, holding on. Her mind went to sleep, a fact I could detect clearly by the softness of her body. I made the same kind of preparation, willed my muscles to hold on, and drifted off to sleep myself. We woke when Keeshah's movement altered; he was slowing down.

Rest, he told me.

He stopped, and we dismounted gingerly, stretching the muscles of our legs slowly, so that they would not cramp up on us.

"Water, Keeshah?" I said aloud, projecting with my mind, as well.

Yes, he said, and lapped up the water Tarani poured into my cupped hands. When the long, pinkish-gray tongue had rasped across my palms, taking the last drop of water, the big cat moved several feet away from us and relieved himself. The power of suggestion, added to natural pressures, was too much for us; Tarani and I separated, seeking the scant cover of the scrubby desert bushes.

The three of us met again where we had stopped—it was a piece of desert indistinguishable from any other. Keeshah came over to me and nuzzled my chest. I braced myself as he turned his head and rubbed his nose and forehead across my torso. He was panting lightly from the exertion of the run.

Thank you for carrying both of us, Keeshah, I told him. *Soon we will be home, and you can have a long rest.*

Ask woman, his mindvoice said. *Female, cubs— well?*

"He's asking about Yayshah and the cubs," I told Tarani, who was scuffing sand about with her booted foot, creating a hollow in which to rest. She smiled and joined us, stroking back the fur at Keeshah's neck.

"Keeshah's family is doing very well," she said, "though I cannot say the same for Thanasset's garden."

I laughed, then passed the information along to Keeshah. *Thank woman,* he said, and poked his nose gently at Tarani's midriff in his own gesture of gratitude. Then he left us and curled up in the sand, his back against two of the short, grayish bushes. I was sure that, if we had not been so close, the cat's tan-and-gray coloring would have made him very hard to spot.

"Keeshah says thank you," I told Tarani.

A strange look passed over her face.

"What is it?" I asked.

She put her hand on my arm as if to steady herself, though she showed no signs of dizziness. I covered her hand with my own.

"Is something wrong, Tarani?"

"Not wrong," she said uncertainly. "Only . . . different. I think—I believe—" She broke off with a small laugh. I was relieved to hear it sound normal and real, not bitter or strained. "I am getting to know Antonia," she said, in a firmer voice. "To be more precise, I am learning what she knew, and seeing things as she saw them."

We had both napped while Keeshah ran, and I wasn't feeling excessively tired. "Let's allow Keeshah his rest, shall we?" I asked, and took her hand. We walked away slowly, in the direction of the blue line against the horizon that marked the Great Wall. The movement was more pleasant than I had expected; I realized we must have had a long run this time, for me to be so stiff.

We were silent for the first few moments. Her darkfurred head was facing the horizon, but her eyes were not seeing it. I couldn't tell if she were in rapport with Yayshah or merely looking into Antonia's world. I reached for words to help or comfort her.

"It must be startling," I said at last, "to begin to question what you have taken for granted all your life."

Her head turned toward me. "Surely you faced this, too?" she asked.

I shook my head. "It wasn't the same for me," I explained. "I am basically a man from a different world; I've always seen the differences first. It took conscious effort to use Markasset's memories for me to be comfortable here."

"And I am essentially Gandalaran, with the memory and viewpoint of an"—she had to search for a word—"a stranger to disrupt my acceptance of the world I have always known."

"Exactly," I agreed. "What was it that disturbed you a moment ago?"

She looked at the ground. The tan leather of our boots was even paler for the coating of sand garnered from three days in the Kapiral Desert.

"I was wondering what lay beyond the Great Wall," she said.

It was simple statement, a simple thought—to a human. A Gandalaran was never out of sight of the boundaries of the "world," and the night sky was almost continually hidden by the thick cloud cover. Gandalarans had never learned the concept of a planet.

She looked up at me. "Do you know?"

"I wish I did," I said, and felt the tremendous relief of being able to discuss the questions that had plagued me since I had arrived in Gandalara. Tarani listened intently while I talked, not even blinking when I couldn't find a Gandalaran word for the concepts and used the Italian. The language felt strange and very musical in the Gandalaran throat.

When I was talked out, Tarani walked away from me and stared at the Great Wall, her hands braced against her hips. "Antonia remembers nothing like the Great Wall in her home world," Tarani said. "But the sight of the Wall from this distance—it stirs something, Rikardon." She stared for a moment, then shrugged and came back to me. "A memory—a thought—it will come in its own time."

"Are you sure it is Antonia who remembers?" I asked. "Your link to the All-Mind is so strong, Tarani—might you not be subconsciously sharing memory with your own ancestors, who might have stood here and wondered about the strip of blue on the horizon?"

She considered. "It may be that, yes," she said, and sighed heavily. "Mysteries within mysteries." She put her hand on my cheek and caressed it. "I see the burden this has been for you, Rikardon. I see, too, that you were right

10

to keep silence about Antonia. Because of her, I *know* now, I can accept awareness of your strange world. Had you spoken earlier, while I lacked that understanding, my fear of the strangeness would have forced me to deny your truth—possibly even to deny you."

Her fingers glided down my cheek to my neck, played there with a light touch that sent my blood singing. But Tarani wasn't aware of the effect she was creating; she was turned inward, thinking.

"How?" she asked softly. "Why?"

I held her upper arms in my hands, drawing her attention back to my face. "We may never know *how*," I said. "But haven't we been working for *why* for a long time now?"

"You mean the Ra'ira?" she asked. "That might explain why we are here," she said, "but why is it *we* and not two other people with human minds that are not subject to the Ra'ira's power? That is—I mean to say, why were you brought here?"

I'm sure my mouth dropped open. "Do you mean to say that you know why *you* were brought here—Antonia, that is?"

"I—well, of course not. I only suggest there may have been a certain logic to choosing Antonia. Her memories show it clearly: she was to die within a few moons of an incurable internal infection."

The wave of grief took me by surprise, so that I staggered back from Tarani. She followed me, concerned. "It's ridiculous," I said, "but I am stunned and sorry—she was so *young*, Tarani, not at all like me."

"Like you?" she said.

"I had heard my own deathbell toll. But I was older, and my life had been full. It could not hurt me so much as it must have hurt her."

Tarani was silent for a moment, reaching into the well of strange memory. "More and more," she said, "I come to admire this woman. She was hurt, yes, but not beaten. She put the knowledge aside and resolved to live her life as normally as possible, asking for no pity, allowing no regrets. She had pride and strength, this one."

"As does this one," I said, taking her face in my hands and leaning forward to kiss it.

11

2

Keeshah ran another long session, covering the miles with amazing speed. At other times, I had guided his run/rest cycle to coordinate with ours, or to conserve his strength. This time, however, I owed him a long rest when we got to Raithskar. I let him set his own pace, knowing he would not extend himself past his capabilities. Tarani and I clung to his back, allowing ourselves to be lulled by the flowing front-to-back rocking motion, at least as much as the need to hang on would allow.

When Keeshah stopped again, the grayish bushes had a touch of green in their scrawny leaves. He was panting heavily. *Need sleep,* he told me, apologizing.

The concept of "sleep," as opposed to "rest," and the tone of apology I sensed from him told me something I didn't want to know. I moved along his side, combing sand out of his fur with my hands.

Keeshah, you've pushed yourself too hard. And there's only one reason why you'd do that—because you thought I wanted it.

You want home, he said.

I felt a twisting jolt of guilt. It wasn't the first time Keeshah had read my feelings more accurately than I could. It *was* the first time it had resulted in possible harm to the big cat. Keeshah had not eaten in three days. That would hardly kill him; he had a capacity for storing food and water that matched the size of his body. But now was not the time to be pushing him hard, when his reserves were low.

12

I wrapped my arms around his neck.

Thank you, Keeshah, I said. *We'll take it easy from here on out, all right? Want some water?*

I gave him another double handful of water, which left Tarani and me with barely a day's ration. She didn't object. She came up to us after Keeshah had lain down, while I finished combing the exposed side.

"He is weary," she said. "Will he let me help?"

I asked Keeshah. *Will you let Tarani help you sleep deeply?*

Yes, he replied, lifting his head to look at Tarani. *Grateful.*

I nodded, and stepped away as Tarani took my place beside Keeshah. The sha'um pressed the side of his face against Tarani's hand, then lay his head on the ground and closed his eyes. Tarani settled herself in a kneeling position. Her hands stroked the big cat, and her voice rose and fell in a gentle, tuneless hum. I felt myself following the sound of it, letting it carry my thoughts into a soothing pattern which slowed gradually. . . .

I had to move away from them before I also fell into the deep, healing sleep Tarani's hypnotic power could engender. When Keeshah was out, Tarani joined me and we stretched out among some bushes.

"It is not like Keeshah to overtire himself," Tarani said. "He must be very eager to reach Yayshah." She must have felt me tense up, because she asked: "What is wrong?"

"I've been pushing him," I admitted. "Without meaning to—but pushing him, just the same."

I didn't need to do any more explaining than that. Tarani had been the one to point out to Thymas and me that she could read our true feelings through the actions of our sha'um. She was quiet for a long time.

"We have had a moment for ourselves," she said at last. "But I have felt it myself—the need to be active again, to continue with this task that has been so strangely set for us." She touched the hilt of the King's sword. "I must take this to Eddarta, as soon as Yayshah and the cubs can make the trip."

"Have you any idea when that will be?" I asked, perhaps a little too sharply.

13

"Has Yayshah not endured enough hardship for our sakes?" she said. "Displaced from the Valley, deprived of a den, and forced to travel throughout her pregnancy? I will not ask her to move again until she assures me she is willing."

I bit back another sharp remark and tried to understand her feelings. "I don't mean to push you, love," I said. "It's only that I have been thinking of the vineh. Because the Council controlled them and bred them for city workers, there are many more of them close to Raithskar than a natural colony would have produced. Free of the Ra'ira's control, they're reverting to their wild state. You remember what they were like outside of Sulis."

She nodded and shuddered slightly. Two sha'um and three people against twenty disagreeable, adult male vineh. We had won—barely. Thymas and Ronar, his sha'um, already weakened, had taken the worst damage and had been quite some time recovering, even with the help of Tarani's healing sleep.

"These aren't quite that bad—they're out of the habit of being nasty. The ones we ran into on the way out of town were easier to deal with than the Sulis group. But it won't take much time before they're a real threat to the safety of the people in and around Raithskar."

"I understand that you feel a loyalty to your people," Tarani said.

Something in her tone made me say, "They are your people now, too."

"I have no *people* in that sense," she said. "Volitar trained me to a life view that allows me nothing in common with Zefra and Indomel, my true family—for which I can only be grateful. Knowledge of my heritage and this present task prevents me from accepting the comfort of Thanasset's home as my own. I have you, and Yayshah, and now this sword."

I held her close for a moment, distressed by what she had said, but unable to comfort her.

"It's not only that I'm afraid for them," I said. "I'm impatient because I feel responsible and committed, and because I can't do anything for them. The next step is

14

yours, and your movement is restricted by consideration for Yayshah. I don't question the rightness of it, Tarani; it just makes me uncomfortable, caught between the need to go and the need to stay, with no real power to choose."

She spoke with her head against my chest. "As always, it is better when we speak truly and frankly," she said. "I know that Yayshah would be quite comfortable staying in Raithskar until the cubs are fully grown. I also know that her desire is born of the instincts and habits she has already abandoned, and she must adapt to the needs of her family—and I include us, as well as Keeshah, as her family. I promise I will judge the time to leave by when she and the cubs are fit to travel, and not by when Yayshah is ready to leave, which she may never be."

"That's fair," I said. "Meanwhile, I'll try to control this itchy feeling and be civil to you."

I felt her smile. "Will you sacrifice so much?" She didn't wait for an answer, but asked another question. "How much further to Raithskar?"

"Keeshah has covered a lot of ground," I replied. "I think Raithskar is no more than half a day away from here."

"Then let us also rest," she said, and started rocking her body to wear a form-fitting groove in the sand. I did the same, until we lay side by side, separated by a few inches of sand, our hands joined. "A long, true sleep will bring us more refreshment than the brief rests we take as Keeshah runs." She sighed. "I look forward to being with Yayshah when she is again sleek and able to run. Already, she has the same longing."

I squeezed her hand.

"The two of you are a pretty impressive pair," I said.

Night came and went while we slept. It was Keeshah who woke first. He roused us by belly-creeping until his head was on the ground, inches away from us, and letting go with his loud bass roar. Tarani and I shot straight up off the ground. Our waking minds rapidly processed the initial perception of danger into the anger-relief reaction of realizing it was a joke, but not before we had nearly strained something trying to get our swords out in the split-second of time while we were reacting and not thinking.

Keeshah, that wasn't funny! I said—but I was laughing. I was also shaking.

15

Home soon, he said. *Glad. Hurry.*

He butted his head between us and swung it, knocking us apart. A paw swept out at me; even though I had a flash of warning and tried to dodge, the clawless swat caught the backs of my legs and knocked them out from under me. He tried the same trick on Tarani, but she was forewarned and jumped to avoid Keeshah's slash.

I could feel Keeshah's delight; he abandoned me and went after her. Tarani, her body trained for both dance and sword, skipped and dodged his swings. The sha'um had such speed that he could have run right over her, but he accepted limits to the game and merely stayed within range to be able to knock her for a loop, if he could only connect. Tarani was laughing with all the joy of a child playing with a kitten. I felt warmed by Keeshah's good mood and the feeling of *family* watching them play together gave me.

Keeshah swung his right paw, and Tarani ran in on the sha'um's right side, sprang off on both feet, and vaulted over his back. The move surprised Keeshah, and in trying to keep her in sight, he twisted himself off balance, fell, and rolled over. He surged to his feet and they faced each other warily, catching their breath.

Suddenly, Tarani lay down on her side, grabbed her knees and tucked her head down against them. Keeshah crouched, all claws out and dug into the sand, ready to move in any direction. She lay motionless, and I thought: *Tarani never played with a kitten and a ball; this idea came from Antonia's memories. It's about time Tarani got something she can really appreciate from her association with Antonia.*

Keeshah crept up on the curled-up Tarani, his tail whipping back and forth, sweeping up an occasional puff of sand. He patted her tentatively with one paw, drawing back twice before he actually touched her; she rocked a little, but kept her pose. He swung with a little more strength, and she rolled over her arms to rest facing the other way, still curled. He tucked his nose under her head and sent her into a lopsided somersault.

I could sense Keeshah's appreciation of the toy Tarani presented him as he came forward more confidently, and I

16

laughed at the shock he felt when she unfolded suddenly and grabbed his head. He retreated backward, dragging her twenty yards or so through the sand and scrub brush, then pinned her body with a paw and pried her off of his neck. He was still in that pose, one paw resting on Tarani's waist, when his head and neckfur lifted simultaneously and he called the warning: *Danger.*

Keeshah whirled to face north, his head high and questing for the source of what he had scented. Tarani hadn't heard Keeshah's mental warning, but she couldn't mistake his reaction. She was on her feet immediately, the steel sword in her hand. I saw her look down at it, momentarily surprised by its different weight and balance.

I had my sword ready, too, and was running to join Keeshah and Tarani when vineh seemed to boil up out of the sand.

The Gandalaran deserts looked flat, but weren't. The ground has a rolling quality, rising into low hills and falling into shallow depressions. Let a few bushes take root in a hill and, even though there is nothing taller than waist-high as far as you can see, there is a respectable amount of cover for someone—or something—wanting to hide. And the pale tan of a vineh's curly fur was further desert camouflage.

The vineh had stalked us with a cunning I had to respect. They had approached from downwind, creeping to within fifty yards of us without alerting Keeshah to their presence. I counted fifteen before I got too busy to worry about it.

Almost as many as we faced near Sulis, I thought. *And we're one man and one sha'um short. But we also have more experience.*

I slashed up at the face of the nearest vineh; he flinched back, and I carried the momentum of the swing around and down, slicing into a leg and bringing the huge apish thing down. As Rika's point slashed across his throat, I sensed another behind me and dropped into a crouch, avoiding the long, reaching arms. I pivoted in the crouch and drove my sword upward, gutting the second beast.

I had a moment to spare, and noticed that a vineh had one of his iron-strong hands clamped around Tarani's left arm. He couldn't take advantage of the hold because she was moving, tugging with her body to keep him off balance.

17

She couldn't deal with him more thoroughly because she was keeping another vineh at bay with her sword, driving him ahead of her with quick, cutting touches.

I was behind Tarani; I brought my sword down on the forearm of the vineh who held her, drew his attention, and finished him. Tarani dispatched the other one, but three more came after us, reinforcements right behind them.

The action had taken us some distance from Keeshah, and the vineh were quick to come between us and the sha'um. *Watch your flanks, Keeshah,* I reminded him. There was no response, only the surge of battle rage that, even more than his formidable weaponry, made the sha'um so dangerous.

They're not harrying him from behind, the way the others did, I thought. *And they're concentrating on us, rather than him. Maybe these "domestic" vineh have accepted Gandalarans as their most powerful enemy. They do seem less hostile generally—if you can call an ape that outweighs you and is trying to kill you unhostile. I wasn't wrong about the ones we met on the way to Kä, either. These are a little awkward, as if their fighting instincts aren't totally reactivated yet.*

Their strategy proved their undoing, because it placed the bulk of the group smack in the middle of a five-point attack machine: my sword, Tarani's sword, and Keeshah (two paws, one set of teeth). The battle was noisy, but the sound had an unreal quality. Keeshah's coughing roar mingled with the snarls and shrieks of the vineh as they fought and fell; I heard both Tarani's voice and my own crying out with the effort of a swing or calling a warning. Yet there seemed to be an unusual quietness, and I finally figured out what was missing: the sound of metal on metal. I was using the muscles and judgment and techniques Markasset developed for fighting armed men, but these were animals, and the only thing our swords struck was flesh.

I wouldn't say that we had never been in danger from this group; it took all our alertness and every bit of our energy to keep away from the strong, horny-nailed hands and the underslung jaws. I will say that, once we had the group in the pincer movement, our defense was well on its way to being a slaughter.

I was glad when one of the larger males, trapped in the center of the group and protected from attack by the bodies of the others, paused and rode out the jostling, looking around. Apparently he saw what he should have seen, because his lips pulled back from the heavy tusks. He barked three short sounds and started battering his way out of the middle, heading for the northern edge of the group.

The others caught on, and all that lay between a potential slaughter and a total rout was opening the pincer.

That's enough, Keeshah, I ordered. *Pull back and let them go.* The sha'um fought on. *Keeshah!* I felt him rising back to rationality through his battle lust. He took one last swipe at a beast already bleeding in a couple of places, and stepped back. His roar of victory followed the vineh.

I looked around, a little stunned by the sudden end of the battle. Pale-furred bodies lay everywhere, leaking dark-red blood into the sand. I felt my stomach turn over, and remembered that Gandalarans seldom vomited; it wasted water, and their evolution had acquired that trait only for dealing with life-threatening situations, just as it had rejected the capability of shedding tears for purely emotional reasons.

Tarani looked grim, too. I took her elbow and called Keeshah to follow as we marched away from the carnage toward Raithskar.

3

We were within sight of the city walls when the vineh attacked again. This time they appeared from grain fields on either side of the main road, which we had been following for the past hour or so. Keeshah became aware of them a second or two before they would have liked, so that they had to leave their hiding places from fifty yards ahead and come after us.

Riding a sha'um during battle might be an advantage, if it could be done. It can't—and there's a much bigger advantage if the sha'um is free to use all its claws without worrying about dumping his riders.

Not that Keeshah was worried about it.

Tarani and I picked ourselves up off the packed dirt of the roadbed. Keeshah had met the group head-on; the fight was tumbling and snarling around him, doing absolutely no good to the edges of the grain fields.

Tarani and I were left to ourselves for a moment.

"Why?" she gasped. "Why are they doing this?"

I just shook my head as we ran to help Keeshah. *They learned from the last battle*, I thought. *They're concentrating on Keeshah this time.*

They had learned more than I expected. Tarani and I were already on the run toward the melee when the edges of the attack group around Keeshah swept around the core of noise and cut us off. Had there been fewer vineh, this might have been a repeat of the pincer victory we had scored in the desert. But still bleeding survivors from the

20

desert battle and fresh "troops" were mixed here, and the vineh had the initiative. A few had picked up farm tools, but the number of vineh was more effective than the occasional swing of a hoe. The beasts pressed Tarani and me back, separating us further from Keeshah.

One of the vineh got past my guard, grabbed for my throat. I flinched back and he caught a big pinchful of flesh and tunic on the left side of my chest. I had my dagger in my left hand; I brought it up under his arm and into his rib cage. Instead of releasing me and going off to sulk, he howled with the pain but held on and jerked me forward. I pulled the dagger out for another stab, feeling the warm blood soak out of his side. We were eye to eye, the vineh and I, at that moment. And I swear that in the bestial eyes, nearly hidden under the prominent supraorbital ridge of his skull, I saw a glimmer of intelligence and a conscious choice as he threw himself on the point of my dagger. I staggered back under the sudden weight, struggling desperately to keep my feet, but failing.

I heard Tarani cry out my name as I went down and the vineh piled on. There were so many of them trying to get a chunk of me that there was no way I could get out from under the dead one, and I used his body as a shield. I was getting bruised pretty badly, but no one vineh could get a solid hold on me. I was reasonably safe but I couldn't breathe. I rocked my lower body until I got my knees under the hips of the vineh, braced by elbows on the ground, and spent what seemed like three years of strain, lifting the vineh's torso a half-inch up, to relieve the pressure on my chest, and gulped in air that reeked of blood.

In that literal breathing space, I felt chilled by what I had seen in the vineh's eyes. An animal throwing itself into danger because it is too enraged to care about its safety is a far different thing from a creature sacrificing itself for the sake of the group's objective. Assuming that I had not merely imagined that glimmer of intelligence, the character of this battle had changed.

The downward pressure lightened suddenly. Buried in vineh, I had been unable to hear anything but their snarling and the pounding of my own heart. The bodies around me were shifting; fresh air penetrated, and with it came sound: Tarani's voice screaming my name, and the coughing roar of the sha'um. *Two* sha'um.

I heaved upward, and the pile of vineh shifted and scattered. Bloody hands helped me shove the dead beast's body over, then helped me to my feet. Distracted by the arrival of the female sha'um from Raithskar, the vineh had left us alone momentarily.

"Are you well?" Tarani asked anxiously.

"I'm fine. Most of this blood isn't mine. What about you?"

"Whole, at least," she said, and her voice cracked. "Rikardon, I feared for you so."

I caught her in a quick, one-armed hug, and looked northward at the battle. The pincer movement was being worked again—this time with two sha'um.

"The cubs?" I asked.

"Well hidden," Tarani said.

Yayshah had circled around and come in from the south, driving the vineh toward Keeshah. Keeshah was holding his own, I was relieved to see. The apes had to climb over their own dead to get close to him. But the long journey, the lack of food, and the strain of this and the recent battle with vineh were telling on him. He was slowing, and the circle of dead vineh restrained him as well as protected him.

Yayshah was fresher and seemed to fight as fiercely as Keeshah, but she was a little slower to begin with because her strength had not fully returned since delivery of her cubs. She was already trampling the dead, pressing toward Keeshah.

One large male launched himself from the dam of bodies around the male sha'um and landed on Keeshah's back. Keeshah screamed as the vineh's teeth dug into the side of his neck; I saw the bloody scoring left by the ape's hands on the sha'um's throat. Keeshah twisted and tucked his head down in almost a bucking motion, but the vineh was fastened on for good. The cat knew better than to try to roll to dislodge the ape; once down, he could never recover the advantage.

Help, he said.

I had pushed Tarani aside and was already running. I

circled to the right and climbed the slippery, unsteady pile of bodies and used myself as a battering ram to knock the vineh loose from Keeshah. We fell into the live vineh, but Keeshah turned our way and kept the others off me until I could finish the one I had grabbed. I scrambled up and joined battle beside him.

Even the vineh are getting tired, I thought. What's keeping them going?

Over the noise of the fighting, I heard a sound that startled me—a high, wailing cry of pain and fear that ended too suddenly. I staggered from an onslaught of feeling from Keeshah, but I hadn't needed that to identify the sound.

One of the cubs had been hurt.

The fighting paused a moment in reaction to the sound, and I hauled myself up to Keeshah's back to see over the heads of the vineh. Tarani was beside Yayshah; both of them facing south. Along the way we had come, five or six vineh had surrounded two terrified and angry sha'um cubs, who had clearly just emerged from the edge of the grain field. The smaller cats were supple and strong. Their teeth weren't fully usable yet, but there was not a thing wrong with their claws, and the two kittens, hip-high to the vineh, were staying free and attacking their captors.

One whitefurred male lay, very still, on the packed dirt of the roadway.

Yayshah screamed, and Tarani jumped with the shock of what Yayshah must have been feeling. But before either of them could take a single step to help, three vineh attacked Yayshah's hindquarters.

Tarani slashed at one of them, but she was getting no help from Yayshah. Concerned more for her cubs than herself, she was dragging the group of them down the roadway, calling frantically to the kittens.

At the sound of their mother's voice, the cubs turned north and tried to run to her. The vineh jumped them, two to a kitten, and pinned them to the ground.

Some of the vineh between Keeshah and Yayshah, free of the trap, streamed out and around the adult sha'um, facing Yayshah from the south and coming in for the attack from Keeshah's rear.

Keeshah's reaction to the danger facing the cubs was so

intense that I couldn't think. I pushed at his mind, reached for his reason through the tide of rage and grief and protectiveness. It was made less easy by the fact that I felt much the same as he did; I was sickly afraid for the cubs. We had gone from a solid attack force to three isolated, surrounded, and vulnerable defense positions. We had to regroup; it was our only hope.

I was still on Keeshah's back, just hanging on while he did all the fighting. He was distracted, worried about the cubs but occupied, moment to moment, with whichever vineh was attacking. They always came in from the rear, of course, so that Keeshah was whirling and turning constantly, tiring even more quickly. He was less disabled by the cubs' danger than Yayshah, but his fighting was less efficient because he was trying to find a way out—to get to the cubs.

The cubs were continuing to take care of themselves pretty well. One—the female, I thought—had crawled forward until her shoulders were free. She twisted with the elasticity of only the very young, and dug her small but sharp teeth into the throat of the vineh. The ape flinched back, and before he could reclaim his grip or hurt the cub, she kicked back, claws out, and got her hind feet free. She backed off from them, her white-tipped kitten fur standing on end, snarling a challenge to the vineh. Her muzzle was bloodied from the vineh's throat.

The male fared less well, but was squirming to the point that the vineh couldn't spare a hand to hurt him and still hold on.

Their fighting instincts are taking over, I thought desperately. *But all that's going to do is get them killed. We need to be together.*

I caught a glimpse of Tarani, bracing herself on Yayshah's back and kicking the face of the vineh clinging to the other side of the sha'um. The scene whirled and danced as Keeshah turned under me, but I saw it when more vineh closed in.

Yayshah went down, and Tarani with her.

We need to be together NOW!

It was a cry of desperation, and the fear and need it carried broke through Keeshah's preoccupation. The sha'um's mind opened and blended with mine, and we,

24

man and cat, became a single unit, reasoning with my mind, fighting with a sha'um's strength. Keeshah stopped his frantic whirling and aimed himself toward Yayshah. He kept three feet on the ground at all times, because I was crouched on his back, using the advantage of height to slash down at any vineh who came close enough to Keeshah's flanks.

Keeshah pushed the vineh back, closing the distance between Yayshah and us. I was relieved to see Tarani's head and shoulders, stable amid the roiling pile of vineh. She still held the steel sword; I watched her lift it high in both hands and bring it down hilt-first on the head of a vineh. Then she was up, slashing and stabbing, fighting to get Yayshah free.

The quality of the battle experience always changed when Keeshah was with me. Odors reached me with head-spinning intensity; sounds were distinct and easily identified as to nature and location; and I always felt imbued with a fierce physical power.

On the other side of the battleground, the cubs had been active. The male was free now, and both were challenging their captors. It was a separate, miniature battle the cubs were fighting, brave and daring, but dangerous to us all. The effectiveness of the adult sha'um depended on the safety of the kittens. Tarani and I would certainly not survive any fight that could beat the sha'um—but I wasn't thinking of that.

I was remembering a furry throat against my thigh, and the rapid, shallow breathing of a young sha'um sleeping.

I was remembering Keeshah lying on the roof of his stone house, his daughter leaning against the wall and batting at the dangling tail.

I was remembering how motionless the third cub seemed, lying white against the dun of the roadbed.

Here! I called, unconsciously projecting the thought as if I were talking to Keeshah.

To my amazement, the cubs paused and looked around, confused. They recovered in time to snarl caution into one of the vineh, who had advanced a bit.

I didn't have to speak to Keeshah; we were blended and he knew what I knew, and what I wanted.

Come to your father, fight with us! I shouted, with my mind and Keeshah's. *Come here!*

The cubs flattened their ears and fur, whirled and made a run for it.

It took the vineh totally by surprise, and they reacted too slowly; they didn't have a chance to catch the kittens. I jumped down from Keeshah's back and cleared out an arc of the circle of beasts around us. The cubs barreled through it the instant it was open.

There was no time for reunions.

Help Keeshah. I directed the cubs, and protected their backs while the three sha'um, buoyed by being together again, steamrollered their way through the vineh that separated them from Yayshah. I felt their surge of joy when the breakthrough came, and their relief that, as soon as the pressure of bodies was gone, Yayshah was able to stand and join them.

Tarani was beside me suddenly, and we turned to face the enemy at the rear together. . . .

The vineh were gone.

4

The vineh were scattering in all directions, half-visible above the waist-high grain in the damaged fields. Once they accepted defeat, they lost no time in abandoning the fight.

The sha'um knew the fight was over, too. As the close link between Keeshah and me faded, I felt both relief and a sense of loss—relief because the blending was an intense experience, and we had held it this time longer than ever before; and loss because I was again limited to my own body and less keen senses. When blended with Keeshah, I felt powerful, invulnerable. I was well aware that the effect was not physical but psychological. When the feeling left, there was nothing to hold off the weariness, and my tired muscles let my body collapse to the ground. I struggled back to a sitting position.

Tarani knelt beside me, her own movements showing the lack of control brought on by great fatigue. She stank with the blood and dust that covered her, and I knew I must look and smell as bad.

"I'm all right," I assured her, patting her hand as it rested on my shoulder. "Just terribly tired."

"Then I will see about the cub," she said, and used my shoulder as a brace to stand up again. I twisted my neck around to look; all the sha'um had moved down the road to gather around the third cub. Tarani walked unsteadily to the group, pushed a cub aside gently, and knelt. I couldn't see the grounded kitten because of all the furry bodies

27

between, but I could see Tarani's face, and I knew the cub was dead.

Yayshah must have taken the message from Tarani's mind at that moment, for she lifted her head and shrieked. The sound began at a painfully high pitch and climbed from there. She held the tone, and Keeshah echoed it at a slightly lower pitch. The children joined in, their voices more raw, with a hissing undertone. The sha'um cried out their grief to the sky while Tarani stood among them, her head bowed.

I thought I would explode with sadness. The sound itself would have been enough. My own grief would have been enough. But I was assaulted and buffeted by the powerful feelings that produced part of that mournful, angry protest from the throats of the sha'um.

What hurt the most was that Keeshah's grief was so like a man's, fraught with guilt. He had lost a child of his body, a creature he was bound, as a father, to protect. He had failed. And there was honestly no blame in him for me. He had left his family to take us into the desert, at my request; had we not gone, he could still be playing contentedly with the children in Thanasset's back yard. With *all* the children.

Through his own grief, Keeshah felt mine, and spared a moment to comfort me. *I chose desert.* His mindvoice was faint and small, as if most of his energy was consumed in his cry, but it came clearly and with unquestionable sincerity. *You saved others,* he said. *Thank you.*

It was only then that I realized I was still in contact with the two living cubs. They had joined the cry in imitation of their parents, and did not understand what they were feeling. Some of it was grief, though they had not truly accepted that their brother was gone. Some of it was fear, born of the intense reaction of their parents. Some excitement and pride over the battle just fought still lingered in the cry too.

They were curious about the voice in their minds.

The wailing reached an almost inaudible pitch, and ceased. A hand touched my shoulder; my mind jumped, but my body was too tired to cooperate.

It was Zaddorn, the Peace and Security Officer from Raithskar, Markasset's friend and rival. He extended his arm and helped me to my feet. Behind him were a troop of men—I would have guessed at least thirty—who were standing as if transfixed, staring at the group of sha'um.

"I am sorry we are too late to help," Zaddorn said, his face grim. "It took a few moments to gather a large enough force."

"You helped," I told him. "They must have seen or smelled you coming, because they gave up suddenly."

He turned to the group of men and gestured forward. "Get started cleaning up this mess," he said. The two columns split around us and went to work dragging the vineh carcasses into piles.

I grabbed one man's arm as he passed. "Don't touch the sha'um," I said. "We'll take care of him."

The man nodded, looking scared, and pried my hand from his arm. It left a bloody mark on the sleeve of his tunic.

"I have never seen so many of them attack at once," Zaddorn said. "And it has been very quiet lately. Rikardon, believe me, if I had even suspected this would happen . . ."

I realized Zaddorn was feeling his own kind of guilt, and I passed along Keeshah's generosity. "There's no way you could have known, Zaddorn. It's the sha'um—vineh hate them." Something about that statement sounded wrong, but I was too tired to figure it out. "Would you mind if we didn't talk just now?"

"Of course not," he said. His gaze shifted behind me.

Zaddorn wasn't wearing the gray hat that marked him in the city. Indeed, now that I looked closely, he was not as carefully groomed as usual. But his manners were intact, and he bowed slightly as Tarani approached us. He said nothing, but transferred my arm, which he had been supporting, into Tarani's grasp.

"We have lost him," she said, and the words seemed to release her control. I held her and let my own grief flow out to mingle with hers. We didn't notice when Zaddorn stepped quietly away.

We walked back into Raithskar between two streams of vlek carts, which had begun hauling the vineh bodies out of the fields. Gandalara was a world that had learned to allow very little to go to waste; the steel forge was not particular about what it used for fuel.

Tarani and I had agreed on a different sort of conservation for the lost cub. We planned to bury him in the ground of Thanasset's garden, where his body would find another kind of life in the beautiful plants it nourished. Keeshah and Yayshah had no objection. Had the cub died in the wild, Yayshah would have buried him where he had fallen.

It had taken both Tarani and me to lift the cub and lay it across Keeshah's shoulders. Keeshah walked between us carefully, and Tarani and I each kept a hand on the cooling body to keep it in place.

Crowds parted silently before us as we entered the city, out of respect for our grief, awe of the sha'um, and fear. The people of Raithskar were not afraid of us, although we must have been a grim and bloody sight. They were afraid of creatures who could destroy a sha'um, the same creatures that had gathered their garbage and repaired their streets. They were afraid of the way things had changed.

Thanasset opened the gate into the yard for us. His sister, Milda, waiting behind him, gasped and turned pale when she saw us. Markasset's father was stunned. He reached out to me and pressed my shoulder. "I am glad to have you home again, son," he said.

It was almost more than I could take. Thanasset knew I was no longer Markasset, yet he cared for me as if I were. I put my hand on his shoulder and couldn't speak.

"We have heard, of course," he said. "There is a bath ready for you."

"Let Tarani use the bathhouse first," I said. "Milda, will you help her? She's exhausted."

"And you are not?" the girl demanded, coming around Keeshah.

I didn't bother to deny it. "Your skills will be needed later, after the sha'um have cleaned themselves up so we can see how badly they're hurt. Get what rest you can now."

She nodded, and we all moved through the gate so that Thanasset could close it against the silent crowd of onlookers. It was made like most things of wood in Gandalara, with layers and layers of small pieces of wood laminated together. When Thanasset closed the gate, I noticed that the inside was badly scarred, with two or three layers missing in spots.

Tarani helped me lift the dead cub from Keeshah's back and lower it to the ground, then she stood up, staggering. Milda—short, stocky, and balding—put her arm around Tarani's waist, tense with concern.

Tarani smiled wearily. "Thank you, Milda. I will appreciate your help."

They moved off toward the back of the yard, where a reservoir on the roof of the bath-house held sun-warmed water ready for bathing. I sat on the ground and stared at the dead kitten. Thanasset sat beside me quietly.

The adult sha'um had moved away, each pinning a cub to the ground and licking it clean. The cubs protested weakly, then relaxed. They were asleep in minutes—two tiny warm presences in my mind. When the cubs were damp and shiny—and remarkably unhurt, I was glad to see—the adults began to groom one another.

"I would have kept the cubs," Thanasset said at last, "but she would not trust me with them. She was wild to go; she even tried to claw her way through the gate." I remembered the scarring. "When I realized she was determined, and might hurt herself trying to get out, I opened the gate for her. She herded the cubs with her. I knew, of course," he said, "that Tarani was in danger. But I never thought Yayshah would take the cubs into battle with her."

"She didn't," I said. "They were hidden in the fields, and I'm sure she ordered them to stay put. The vineh spotted them and attacked." I looked up into the old man's face, more lined than it had been a few days ago. "They dragged the cubs out into the road, where we could see them. And as I think of it now, they weren't trying very hard to hurt them."

"What are you saying?"

"I'm saying that they dragged the cubs into it to divide us and demoralize us. It worked."

"That's not possible," the old man said, showing real fear for the first time since I (as Ricardo or Rikardon) had known him. "You forget—" he began, then lowered his voice. "You

31

forget that I have known their minds. They are beasts, I tell you; they are not capable of such reasoned planning."

"Wild vineh aren't, I grant you that," I said. "But these are the product of generations of inbreeding and behavior control that rewarded them for their successful imitation of men. They learned to sweep streets because someone showed them how. Why should that be the only thing they learned?"

"They were not taught tactics," he said sharply.

"You said you've touched their minds; you know how they think," I said. "Couldn't that work both ways? Couldn't they have learned how *you* think?" He looked so horrified that I added: "In general terms, I mean. Couldn't they know, for instance, that although we live in large groups, we are more bound to family than to colony, and that we are each protective of our own young?"

He considered that for a few minutes, his hand stroking the soft fur that covered the stiffening body in front of us.

"I suppose it could be true," he admitted. "But I have no wish to believe it. It paints the vineh in the role of a true enemy of Raithskar, rather than a nuisance to be controlled. If they can summon such numbers against a few, can we expect an all-out attack on the city?"

"I doubt it," I said. "Zaddorn said it's been fairly quiet, and I assume he meant that the 'escaped' vineh haven't been giving anybody much trouble."

"That's true," Thanasset said. "The Council agreed to leave the grain fields and a herd of glith west of the city unguarded, so the vineh would have no need to fight for food. It has kept confrontations to a minimum—until today."

"Today doesn't count," I said. "I think the sha'um triggered the attack." I felt the same nudge of oddness that I felt talking with Zaddorn, but I was able to identify it now. "It's possible the vineh didn't even realize it. There were two battles, you know—"

"Two battles?" he asked.

I took a few minutes and described both battles we had fought that day against the vineh. I tried to keep my emotions out of the description, but Thanasset made up for it by putting in his own while he listened. He looked thoroughly shaken by the time I finished.

"I am afraid I still do not understand what you mean," he said.

"I think the sha'um and the vineh are natural enemies," I told him. He looked blank, and I tried to explain. "Sometime in the past—a *long* time in the past—the wild vineh and the wild sha'um may have been constantly fighting one another. It went on long enough that the young were born with an awareness of danger in the other species. That awareness never went away."

"But Keeshah was never bothered," Thanasset said. "My sha'um was never bothered."

"Because the vineh inside Raithskar were not in a natural state," I said. "Your control blocked that instinct as effectively as it blocked their tendency toward violence. I think they attacked us in the desert because the sha'um triggered that instinct—but because the bulk of their conscious experience with enemies lay with men, they concentrated on Tarani and me. By the time they launched the second attack, they knew who they were really fighting."

"It makes a kind of sense," he said. "Does it not mean, however, that they will persist in trying to reach the sha'um and destroy them?"

"I'll grant them cunning," I said, "but not intelligence. They went after Keeshah because his scent stimulated their aggression. The scent of sha'um is lost in the center of Raithskar. And we won't leave the city again until we're ready to leave for good."

"Back to Eddarta," Thanasset said. "I saw the sword · Tarani carried. Did it—have the effect you anticipated?"

I had confided in the old man that Tarani was a "visitor," which was exactly what he understood me to be—a personality returned from the All-Mind to inhabit a living body. It was a concept he could comprehend, and it was as close to the truth as I dared get. Tarani, even with Antonia's memories to help her, had a hard time accepting the real truth of the world from which we had come.

I nodded. "The union took a different form with Tarani," I said. "She is herself, with the memories of the visitor." I stood up a little awkwardly—my sore muscles had stiffened while I was sitting. "I have a lot to tell you," I said, "but there is something I need to tend to first. We—" I choked up suddenly. "May we bury Yayshah's cub in your garden?"

"I will be honored," he said, and went to get his digging tools.

5

My prediction of no further trouble proved, thankfully, to
be true. Tarani and I and the sha'um went on vacation for a
while, resting deeply. Milda fussed over us pleasantly and
fed us constantly. Thanasset took charge of providing food
for the sha'um; already Yayshah was chewing up bits of
meat and leaving it for the cubs to work on, and their
chewing action was stimulating the full emergence of their
teeth.

Tarani's hypnotic skill hastened our physical healing to a
degree that amazed Milda. Yayshah was the only one who
had been immobilized long enough to suffer from the teeth,
as well as the hands, of vineh. She had some painful gashes
in her back and flanks, and some ugly scars in the paler fur
of her still-tightening underbelly. Keeshah carried more
wounds, but they were mostly surface scratches, quickly
covered with new fur growth.

Tarani and I needed new skins. I had reexperienced the
pain when Thanasset had helped me peel off my blood-
soaked clothes and bathe open the myriad of scratches.
Milda smeared us daily with a skin salve to keep the newly
forming scabs soft. After a few days of looking like walking
horror-film monsters, the ridges of skin softened and
closed, and finally dropped off to leave behind little more
than faint marks in our skin.

The wound left by the cub's loss didn't heal, but the pain
faded as we took pleasure in the other two. They were,
indeed, nearly unharmed, which seemed to confirm my

feeling that the vineh who had held them had not been trying to hurt them.

"Why did they kill the other one?" Tarani asked me one day, as we watched Yayshah rolling in the shade of the sha'um house, offering her paws as targets for the cubs' stalking practice. Keeshah was in his favorite spot, snoozing on the roof of his house.

The kittens were growing with a wild speed, leaving behind the pale-tipped fur of their babyhood. The male, whom we had named Koshah, looked like a smaller duplicate of Keeshah, right down to the nearly indistinguishable pattern of pale tan against pale gray in his fur. He was already bigger than his sister, with slightly awkward proportions that promised he would match Keeshah's size, which was unusually large among sha'um.

The female, Yoshah, moved with delicate grace, attacking any target with economy of movement and unerring accuracy. She was brindled like her mother, striped in varying shades of dark gray and brown. In the natural environment of the Valley, the markings would provide camouflage. Outside the cooler, highly overgrown Valley, however, the darker coats brought more discomfort from the heat to Yayshah and Yoshah than the males suffered.

"I don't know," I told Tarani. "I may be giving them more credit than they deserve. They might have intended to kill the others, too, until they saw the effect the live, crying kittens had on the big sha'um."

"There is another thing I do not understand," Tarani said. "I could spare little attention for anything but fighting, but I do remember a sudden change. One moment, Koshah and Yoshah were fighting their own battle with their captors; the next instant, they had joined Keeshah."

I don't know why I hadn't told anyone about the cubs and me. Perhaps it was only the human tendency to enjoy a secret delight more, on occasion, than a shared pleasure.

The link with the cubs was of a different quality than my link with Keeshah. His was a continuing, comfortable presence often overlooked, like two people who had lived together for so long that accommodation and compromise were accomplished almost automatically on a daily basis. The cubs were volatile, sometimes unaware of me, sometimes offering a mental nuzzling of curiosity, now and then exploding into a full blend—jointly or individually—that brought me the unrestrained joy of romping childhood again. Yet even then, it wasn't the full, binding, total experience that a blend with Keeshah produced.

I had been careful not to exercise the link with the cubs more than to make them aware that I was the body associated with the mind they knew. Sha'um didn't normally bond until they were at least a year old, and I was concerned that this early bonding, brought about by such a traumatic need, would affect their normal development.

I chose to exercise it now, however—by way of explanation to Tarani.

Yoshah, come, I said. *Koshah, come.*

On the roof of the house, Keeshah raised his head. *Me?* he asked sleepily.

No, I call the cubs, I answered him.

Good, he grunted, and went back to sleep.

The two young sha'um broke off the sneak-and-pounce game they were playing with their mother and ran over to the garden bench where Tarani and I were sitting. The male lumbered up, put his forepaws on the stone seat, and lifted his upper body until he was looking down at me. The female barreled straight at us and threw herself on her side at the last minute, arriving with four paws and a set of teeth in contact with my boots.

"Whoa," I said hastily, startled in spite of the fact that I could see from her mind she was only playing. I bent over and uncurled her, stroking her fur with my spread fingers, while Tarani reached over my back to attend to scratching Koshah's ear.

Go on back to your mother now, I told them. Yayshah was sitting up, watching us curiously—a little warily, I thought. *I love you. Have fun.*

They went, Koshah pausing to butt his forehead against my shoulder as he left.

Tarani said: "They are darling creatures, are they not? I find it hard to picture them fighting vineh, though I might draw the image from my own memory. . . ." She stopped, and I knew she had connected back to our interrupted conversation. "You called them," she said. "Just now, and during the fight."

37

"Keeshah was with me during the fight," I said. "I feel sure that's what made it possible—the cubs must have recognized his mind, on some level."

"And when Keeshah left you, when the danger was gone?"

"The link remained."

"With both of them?"

"Yes."

"And what of Keeshah? Is he linked to them directly, as well?"

It was a possibility that had not occurred to me, and I felt myself getting as excited at the prospect as Tarani sounded.

"I honestly don't know," I said, and in my eagerness woke Keeshah up, then and there, to test it out.

Say something to the cubs, I asked him, when he had grumbled awake. There was an unflattering picture in his mind of a crazy two-legged creature, but he complied. He snarled. The cubs jumped, and looked up curiously. Yahshah snarled back.

Not like that, I said. *Say something to them the way you talk to me.*

Keeshah squirmed on the rooftop until his head lay across one paw. His silver-flecked eyes glowed as he blinked slowly at me.

Silly, he said, and closed his eyes.

I knew that mood; it was no use trying to rouse him now.

"He won't even try," I said to Tarani, exasperated.

"I am rather glad," she said, surprising me. "Look at it from Yayshah's point of view," she explained. "Would you care to try to teach a child who could learn any needed thing directly from the mind of his father?"

"It might be hard," I admitted.

"And it is hard enough to know that you can speak to them; I would feel even more deprived if Keeshah had acquired the ability, as well."

I took her hand, and we sat quietly for a while. I was feeling nearly fit, after all the rest and attention I'd been enjoying. I was feeling fit enough, in fact, to be a shade restless. Thanasset had forbidden us visitors until we were healthy again, and I knew nothing of what was happening in the city except what Thanasset brought home, and that was usually a relieved announcement that no vineh attacks had occurred that day.

"How's your leg doing?" I asked Tarani suddenly. Her most severe wound had been four lacerations dug from the outside of her right thigh by the nails of a vineh hand. She had limped a bit the first few days, but I hadn't noticed the limp lately.

"It is nearly healed," she said. "Why do you ask?"

"I think we deserve a little fun, as well as a lot of rest, don't you."

"Yes, but—" she began, bewildered.

"Come out with me tonight," I urged her. "Dinner first, and then dancing. We'll pretend we have nothing to do but have a good time."

Her face lit up like a child's; she laughed out loud and threw her arms around my neck.

"It is exactly what I want to do," she said, and kissed my ear, sending a tingle down my chest. "I did not know I wanted it until you spoke. But yes, please, I want to dance again."

Tarani disappeared for the rest of the day. I played with the cubs, harassed Milda in the kitchen, napped, and finally bathed and dressed for the evening. Daytime dress in Gandalara was a haphazard sort of thing—usually long-sleeved or sleeveless tunics, with trousers added for adults if the tunic's hem hit midthigh or higher. The most common fabric was made of a woven grain floss, the cost inversely proportional to the tightness of the weave. Raithskarians had a fondness for bright colors and were not particular about how they were combined. If you bothered to wear colors that matched or complemented each other, you were getting dressed up.

Markasset had enjoyed dressing well, so that I had a lot to choose from. I looked at, but rejected, the green outfit I had worn when I had taken Illia dancing back in my "innocent" days, when I had not known the truth about the Ra'ira. The outfit reminded me of my hope, long since abandoned, of being able to settle into a quiet and contented routine in which to live this strangely acquired second life.

I refolded the green outfit and put it on one of the higher shelves in Markasset's closet. Digging around the back of the lower shelves yielded an unusual garment: a sleeved shirt of pale yellow, hip length, styled like a vest but large enough to wrap. I tried it on, looked into the polished bronze of a mirror, and decided Markasset must have saved this for very special occasions. The color accentuated the dark gold of my headfur; the opening exposed a long "V" of curly-haired chest. I found some trousers of a warm brown color and a matching vest. The vest belted to form a second "V" over the pale yellow shirt. I was satisfied that I looked special enough for my first date with Tarani.

I went downstairs, and realized that I had begun to take my union with Markasset's memories for granted. Thanasset was just coming in, and it wasn't until his face registered shock that I identified the "special occasion" for which Markasset had saved the open-necked shirt. It was intended to be nightwear—*wedding* nightwear. Markasset had bought it while thinking about Illia.

But I chose it, thinking about Tarani, I told myself, pausing on the stairs. *What the hell . . . I don't have a reputation for being normal in this world; why change now?*

I stepped down to the wood parquet floor of the house's center hallway and touched Thanasset's shoulder in greeting. His face was a study in embarrassment: Does he know? Should I tell him? What can I say? Will it embarrass him?

Before I could say something to make him less uncomfortable, I heard a sound on the stair behind me. Thanasset's face took on a whole new expression, and I knew when I turned that I would see Tarani.

She was something to see.

And I thought I was going to some trouble to look nice tonight, I thought. *No wonder I haven't seen her at all today. She must have spent the whole day shopping and sewing.*

From the corner of my eye, I caught a movement in a doorway down the hall. Milda was hovering there, peeking around the corner.

Dear Aunt Milda, I thought. *She must have had a lot of fun today, helping and keeping the secret.*

From the multitude of fabric colors available in Raith-skar, Tarani had chosen black. Her outfit was made up of a loose, bell-sleeved tunic and full-legged trousers. The high collar and hem of the tunic, as well as the edges of sleeves and trouser legs, were decorated with a pattern made up of hundreds of small, shiny black beads.

There's no way she could have sewn each of those beads in the time she had, I thought. *Someone must specialize in making beaded trim.*

Tarani smiled when she saw us, and did a small turn down the last three steps. Like the blue gown she had designed for her performances, her new outfit was designed to enhance the movements of dancing. The material draped in graceful folds as she walked, but swirled out at hips and ankles when she turned her body. The lightly weighted hems were responsive to her every movement.

Thanasset still had his mouth open. Milda couldn't stand it; she came from the dining room to join us in admiring Tarani.

The girl's looks came from her genetic link to the Lords of Eddarta, and were very rare on this side of the Morkadahls. She was tall, with very dark headfur that made the widow's peak above her supraorbital ridge much more noticeable. Her cheeks were high, with narrow planes joining them to a small chin. The dramatic outfit enhanced the contrast between her pale skin and silky headfur, and made her black eyes seem larger.

She had the kind of raw beauty that quickened the heart. She had enhanced it artfully, and her glow of pleasure at our obvious admiration added to it. The final touch was the spark of appreciation that lit her eyes when they rested on me.

6

I had taken Illia to the same places I took Tarani that night, but I felt no sense of nostalgia or déjà vu. The women were too different; I wasn't the same man; and the city had changed.

Illia's golden beauty had caught appreciative looks on that other night, but Tarani turned heads wherever we went. It was more than her striking looks and the stunning, dramatic outfit. It was the way she carried herself and kept her attention on me, as if she had no awareness of the sensation she was creating.

She was born to be a queen, I thought, as we entered the Moonrise Restaurant. The next logical thought jolted me so that I must have twitched physically. Tarani felt it through my hand on her elbow, and looked at me with concern. I smiled, shook my head, and we continued following the host to the table he had selected.

Queen of Eddarta, I repeated in my thoughts, as we sat. *All our talk of destiny—we've been assuming that "destiny" brought us together for a permanent alliance. What if we're wrong?*

"Rikardon?" Tarani asked, leaning over the corner of the tile-topped table. "Something disturbs you?"

I put my hand over hers. "Nothing we need to talk about tonight, love," I said.

She looked at the patterns in the tile. "Are you eager to be moving again?" I felt the tension in her fingers. "It should be possible soon. . . ."

I touched her chin with my hand, and she lifted her face to look at me. "I'm eager to do nothing but enjoy this evening, Tarani. I haven't told you tonight—perhaps I've never told you, now that I think of it—how beautiful you are, how proud I am you care for me, how just being with you gives me a sense of wholeness, but not of complacency. You excite my mind, feelings, and my body. I feel challenged and powerful when I'm with you, Tarani, and"—my voice faltered, as I realized what I was saying—"and I never want to *not* be with you again."

She looked stunned, as well she might. I dropped my hand from her chin before she could feel it tremble.

"Your outfit is magnificent," I said, surprised that my smile felt reasonably steady. "I'm sure everyone here appreciates all the work you must have done today."

She started to say something, changed her mind, and went along with changing the subject. She smiled hesitantly at first, then let the smile light up her face.

"You have made it clear," she said, "that *you* appreciate it, which was my only goal. It is generous of you to assume that I am the one who attracts the eyes of the crowd. It takes no special skill to read the envy in the women who watch us."

A hostess appeared, carrying glasses of faen, the Gandalaran equivalent of beer. We placed our orders—I wanted a glith steak; Tarani opted for a vegetable stew dish—and the evening took on one more similarity to the time I had spent with Illia. Now, as then, we shared a willingness to ignore thoughts of past or future in favor of enjoying the moment.

It worked for a while. We ate dinner and walked to the dance hall, hand in hand. Tarani was absolutely delighted with the large, patterned floor, and the people moving rhythmically, in unison, each following the pattern of the specific dance. I was surprised to learn that this type of dancing was unknown outside of Raithskar. The dances themselves were based on dances Tarani knew, but they had been formalized. Movement was linked to the floor patterns, and interaction between the dancing couples had been added. Tempos varied from graceful swaying to an intricate and rapid foot placement that would have put calisthenics to shame.

Each of the tables was numbered and could seat four people. It was still early, so that we were alone at our table. Tarani could barely contain her eagerness until our number was called. We took our place on the multicolored tile, and the music started.

And I thought Tarani turned heads at the restaurant, I said to myself, amused at the sensation the girl in the black outfit was creating.

Tarani danced exactly the same way everyone else danced, incorporating variations with the skill of a trained dancer. Her movements were the same as the other dancers, but the grace of her body and the design of her clothes enhanced them, setting her apart from the ordinary. Knowing we were in the spotlight, literally, I put forth some extra effort to be a better partner for her.

After the dance, some of the nearby couples took the trouble to speak to us, complimenting our dancing. Tarani was positively glowing as we headed back to our table—which was no longer empty.

"Good evening," Zaddorn said, as he stood up. "Illia assured me you would not object to our joining you."

Illia was looking at the table top. I didn't bother wondering why.

"You're welcome, of course," I said. "Tarani, I believe you met Illia outside the house just before we left."

"Yes, I recall it well," she said, nodding at the girl. Then she turned her attention to Zaddorn. "I am pleased to see you, Zaddorn. In the stress of the day we returned to Raithskar, you and I did not meet formally. But I was very much aware of your kindness and concern, and I am grateful for the opportunity to thank you now."

To his surprise and mine, Tarani put out her hand. Zaddorn bowed slightly as he took it. I couldn't miss the eyebrow he raised in my direction. I had been the only other person ever to offer him a handshake.

"I can assure you, you have the sympathy of everyone in the city," he said. "You"—he gestured to include me, as well as Tarani, in his statement—"and your family of sha'um are a center of interest, a spot of joy in an otherwise very frightened city."

44

I had been trying to ignore the signs—laughter just a bit too loud, faen flowing more freely than usual, a frantic quality to the gaiety. I wanted to continue to ignore it, but Zaddorn's expression told me I wouldn't have the opportunity.

Tarani, sensitive as ever, said: "Will you excuse me for a moment? Illia, would you mind showing me where . . ."

Illia looked from Zaddorn's face to mine, and showed more perception than I would have given her credit for. "Of course not—it's this way," she said, as she stood and left the table.

Zaddorn and I sat down, and he wasted no time.

"Had you been accepting visitors," he said, "I would have talked with you long before now. This vineh business, rough as it has been, has not made me forget about the Ra'ira. I presume we would have it now, if you had returned with it. Where is it? What happened?"

I stared at him, surprised. "I told Thanasset everything, and I assumed he passed it all on to the Council."

Zaddorn snorted. "I suspect that's true. What gives you the idea that the Council tells *me* anything?"

"What *have* they told you?" I asked.

He sighed. "They have told me to 'control the vineh.' The day after the attack on you, Ferrathyn came to my office and shouted until his Supervisor friends dragged him away."

"Ferrathyn?" I said. The image of the slight, friendly old man in an apoplectic rage was totally foreign to my memory of the Chief Supervisor. "*Ferrathyn?*"

"He has changed," Zaddorn said. "It would be a lie to say we have ever been friends, but I did think we respected one another. This situation has made him—the best word that occurs to me is *intense*. I fear the strain is making him feel his age, and I find it less and less palatable to concede to the whims of someone I suspect to be unbalanced." He shrugged and sipped his glass of faen. "But then, I suppose I have given him little reason to respect me lately. I have been totally unable to control the spread of the vineh illness, and less than effective in protecting private property from the raids of the wild group."

Ferrathyn must have changed a lot, I thought. *I'd have*

bet that the old man's sense of fairness would insist that Zaddorn be told the truth about the Ra'ira and the vineh, instead of that crock about an ape flu. I don't doubt that Ferrathyn has suffered from the strain—probably from a heavy load of guilt, as much as anything.

Zaddorn was staring into his faen, lost in his own sense of failure.

The Council didn't tell me about the Ra'ira, I remembered. *I had to find out the hard way. But now that I know, do I have the same obligation they do—not to reveal the truth without the Council's consent?*

Zaddorn glanced up, saw my face, and leaned across the table to touch my arm.

"Rikardon, I have seen that look on too many rogueworld faces not to recognize it. If you know something that can help, please tell me."

Markasset had known Zaddorn throughout his youth. They had been rivals in sports and war games and romance. Through it all, Markasset had suffered from a sense of inadequacy, each victory only a reminder of his other losses. Markasset had resented and admired Zaddorn. I, as Ricardo and Rikardon, had shifted that balance toward admiration, even though I was not blind to Zaddorn's irritating qualities. High on that list was arrogance—a quality absent from the vocal tone he had just used to ask for help.

Council or no Council, I decided, *Zaddorn deserves to know the truth. He is being asked to control a situation he's not even close to understanding.*

"I don't know how it will help," I said quietly, "but I will tell you what I know. I ask only two things in return: that you accept what I say as the truth without question, and that you keep your temper under control. There are many reasons why you *haven't* been told this, none of them born of lack of confidence in you. Agreed?"

Zaddorn's face lit up with its normal expression—wry amusement, aloofness, cynicism. "With such an introduction, my curiosity is rampant. Of course, I promise what you ask."

"All right, here it is. The Ra'ira can be used to amplify mindpower. It is and always has been, potentially, a tool for

46

mind control. The early Kings used it to learn and lead better; the later Kings used it to control slaves. Serkajon knew what it was, and brought it here for safekeeping. Generations later, someone hit on the idea of using it to control the minds of animals, rather than men. Of course, the animal had to have something of a mind to begin with, and the accomplishment had to be worth the effort."

"The vineh?" Zaddorn gasped. "Not trained at all, but *controlled*?"

I shook my head. "No, they were controlled only when the training broke down," I said. "Since this stuff got started, a Supervisor has been on duty with the Ra'ira every hour of every day. I guess you could say they watched the vineh minds for signs of rebellion, and controlled it out of them when it was found."

"And when the Ra'ira was taken away . . ." Zaddorn's voice trailed off. His hand balled into a fist, and he raised it to hit the table. I caught his wrist just in time to save the faen glasses from a dangerous bouncing.

"You promised," I reminded him.

He tensed as if he might use his other fist on my face, then opened his hand. I let my hand ride his wrist to the table, and kept it there—I had detected no signs of relaxation or resignation. I felt him pressing on the table's surface.

"You do not know," he said, "the charade they have put me through. Moving half the colony to another location, to avoid spreading the 'disease.' My men hurt often at the beginning because they were expecting only as much violence from the beasts as they had seen before—which had never blossomed fully, as you now tell me. All the scorn and blame heaped on me, when I was not given the basic truth of the situation."

His hand was still tense; I could almost feel anger coursing in the pulse I felt at his wrist.

"You have it now," I said. "Does it help?"

His gaze snapped up from the table to meet mine. "To know that I have changed one situation out of my control for another? You tell me the Ra'ira is the cause—and, I assume, the cure—of the vineh situation. Its return to Raithskar seems to have been left up to you. *Where is it?*"

47

It took an effort of will to keep from flinching away from Zaddorn's accusing gaze. "The Ra'ira is in Eddarta," I said. "Tarani is the key to getting possession of it, and she is as committed as I am to delivering it back to Raithskar."

"When?"

"I can't say for sure. We have to get there, and back again. And we will need some time *in* Eddarta—it's complicated, Zaddorn."

"Several moons, then?" he asked.

"At least," I said.

"And meanwhile?" he demanded. "The attack on you involved a huge group of the beasts. If that is a sign of their activity, in 'several moons' you may not find Raithskar here when you return."

"It won't be that bad, once we're gone," I said, and told him my theory about the sha'um stirring instinctive enmity in the vineh. "And you're alert now to the possibility that the vineh can use some strategy when they fight. Being forewarned should help a little."

Zaddorn's tenseness had faded as we talked. I released his wrist and he sat back in his chair. His face went blank, and he stared over my shoulder.

He's planning defenses, I thought. *I hope the Council is aware of this man's value.*

Tarani and Illia came back to the table. Illia's hand on Zaddorn's shoulder startled him back to the present. She glanced at me, then leaned down to whisper in Zaddorn's ear. He put his hand over hers and grinned wryly at me.

"Illia reminds me of the reason we joined you this evening, Rikardon," he said. "We want you to know that Illia and I shall marry soon. May I say that I hope you will not be able to attend the ceremony?"

"Zaddorn!" Illia gasped.

The golden-furred girl's face was a study in shock and embarrassment. "Rikardon, he does not mean that, he—" she stammered.

Behind Illia, Tarani was merely watching and listening. I stood up, touched one hand to the pair of hands on Zaddorn's shoulder, and kissed Illia's cheek—and reached around Illia to take and press Tarani's hand.

"Illia darling," I said, "Zaddorn knows I will probably be

leaving Raithskar before your wedding. I trust you know that I wish you both all happiness."

"Leaving?" Illia said.

"Yes. Tarani and I must return to Eddarta."

Illia twisted a bit to look at Tarani, and her glance saw our hands, joined behind her back.

"Oh," she said, then, with a slightly confused sincerity, added, "I—I am happy for you, too, Rikardon."

7

"It was a lovely evening," Tarani whispered, as we opened the gate into Thanasset's garden.

I closed the gate, staggering a little. My legs felt like thinly stretched rubber.

I wasn't this tired after my three-day run from the Lingis mine to Eddarta, I thought.

Tarani, too, seemed happily tired. We leaned on each other as we moved through the semi-darkness. In the desert, the moonless sky would have left us in blackness; in the city, the all-night glow of the entertainment district provided some illumination.

We made our way to the stone house at the back of the yard. The blackness inside the sha'um house was complete. We couldn't see or touch them, and we had only to "look" with our minds to know they slept, but Tarani seemed to share my impulse to be close to the sha'um for a moment. We leaned on the wall of the house.

Keeshah's presence came to me, large and warm and somnolent. The two cubs were there, too—each a lighter presence, as if weight in body and experience were reflected in a kind of mental mass. I was pervaded with a sense of *family*, and felt so full and rich that I couldn't catch my breath.

Tarani felt it, too, and came into my arms as I reached for her. "I see from Antonia's memory," Tarani whispered, "that dancing is different in your world. I wish to learn."

In spite of the fatigue in my legs, I drew her out into a

50

clear area of the garden, caught her hand, pulled her close against me, and hummed. The tune had silly romantic lyrics that ran through my head as we swayed together. The tune and dancing together, bodies touching, had been unknown in Gandalara until that moment, yet sharing them with Tarani, combined with the comforting awareness of the sha'um made me feel, for the first time, totally and entirely a part of Gandalara. The feeling shimmered while we danced, then faded back from the force of its natural consequence: a renewed commitment to the task I had accepted.

In my mind, Keeshah's presence stirred, then slipped back into sleep. Tarani stopped dancing; I pulled away to look into her face.

"I cannot read your thoughts," she explained, "but I am learning to know your moods. I am ready to leave Raithskar as early as tomorrow." I could barely see her face well enough to notice her smile. "I agreed to see Illia this evening, for a conference on dress design."

"The cubs are ready to travel?"

"Can you not tell that better than I?" she asked, a little sharply.

"The cubs are *ready* for anything," I said. "They have no way of knowing what they *can* do until they try."

"Of course, I should have realized that," she said. "I apologize, Rikardon. I have no right to envy your link with the children, when the forging of that link probably saved their lives."

"I guess the big question is, will Yayshah leave?"

Tarani nodded. "I think so. She is fretful. The house is the closest thing she has seen to a suitable den and she loves it, but the garden lacks room for them to run. I sense a need in her to train the cubs, yet an awareness that it is unnecessary when food is provided without effort."

"Tomorrow, then," I said. "We'll go back the way we came, along the edge of the Morkadahls. Most of the time, the sha'um will be able to hunt their own food."

Tarani peered at me through the gloom. "I hear no eagerness in your voice, Rikardon. Yet you wish to go, I know that well. Please tell me what troubles you."

"I'm not sure," I said, and it was largely true.

51

"Is it leaving your home?" she asked gently.

"My home," I said, pulling her close again, "will be going with me."

After dinner that evening, Tarani left for Illia's house. Milda went with her, intending to visit a friend who lived in the same area. Thanasset and I were settled in the sitting room with tiny glasses of barut when someone knocked at the door.

"I'll get it," I said, setting my glass down on the table and trying to heave my dinner-sated body out of the armchair.

"Stay there," Thanasset said, laughing. "You ate as if you never expected another meal. I shall answer the door."

He left the room. I heard laughter out in the midhall and Thanasset returned with a small man who looked frail and old. I tried to stand up again, but the old man smiled, wreathing his face in wrinkles, and waved me back.

"Sit, Rikardon, sit," he said, and looked me up and down. "Thanasset said you have been doing Milda's cooking justice since you returned. As thin as you still are, I am just as glad I did not see you immediately." The smile faded. "I would have grieved heavily for your suffering on our behalf."

He lowered himself into a chair.

"I shall not try to be subtle, my friends," the old man said. "I have come to ask you bluntly, Rikardon, whether the Council should make preparations to fight Eddartans, as well as vineh."

Thanasset looked startled and confused. I understood how he felt.

"Surely, Chief Supervisor, you don't think—your letter— Tarani wishes only—"

It was Ferrathyn's turn to look shocked, then he laughed.

"Oh, no, my boy—as you trust the lady Tarani's motives, I can do no less. My concern is with the Ra'ira and its present danger to us. I have heard something of Eddarta and its rulers in my lifetime, and nothing good of Pylomel or his son. Indomel has the Ra'ira, yes?"

"Yes," I said, "but there's no need to be concerned about danger from Eddarta, for two reasons: First, Indomel hadn't figured out how to use the Ra'ira by the time Tarani

52

and I left Eddarta. Second, he's greedy, but fairly practical. Only a raving madman would consider trying to rebuild the Kingdom with the world as it is today."

Ferrathyn's head snapped up at that, and he seemed to start to say something, then think better of it.

"I know," I assured him, "Gharlas was that kind of a madman. If he had lived and kept the Ra'ira, Raithskar would have cause to worry about an attack from Eddarta."

"Then there is no danger from Indomel?"

I shook my head. "For one thing," I said, "as far as I know, he hasn't yet learned the trick of using the Ra'ira. For another, he has small ambitions. All he wants is more power over the other Lords."

Thanasset stepped in, sounding anxious. "There is no trick to using the Ra'ira," he said. "New Supervisors learn it quickly."

"New Supervisors," Ferrathyn reminded him, "have someone to teach them."

"Indomel wanted Tarani to help him learn," I said. "I think it was the main reason he let her stay alive."

"Then the lady Tarani *can* use the stone's power?" Ferrathyn asked quietly.

"We're not sure of that," I told him. "She was able to read the inscription on the Bronze while she was holding the Ra'ira, but she can't say whether it was her natural ability, the stone's power, or her training as a Recorder that let her do it so easily."

Ferrathyn looked at Thanasset with mock seriousness. "This detail of her being a Recorder—you failed to tell me that, my friend."

Thanasset smiled. "I warned you the story would be clearer from Rikardon. Yet you chose to take my second-hand account—"

"Thanasset told me your joints were troubling you," I said to Ferrathyn, smiling at the interplay between the old friends. "I'm glad you felt well enough to come this evening. Should your trouble return on the next occasion, Tarani and I would be honored to come to you."

"The honor would be mine," the old man said. "I regret that I have missed meeting the next High Lord of Eddarta, yet again. Do you see any difficulty in her enforcing her claim?"

I opened my mouth, closed it again, and then laughed.

"I *see* no difficulty," I said. "We have the King's sword, and her mother's support, and the weight of the other Lords' dislike for Indomel on our side. But if difficulties could be anticipated, they would cease to be difficulties, wouldn't they?"

Both men laughed with me, but I could see their hearts weren't in it. Ferrathyn, in fact, looked a little ill. A slight tremor stirred the long sleeves of his tunic, where his wrists lay along the arms of the chair.

"It will be several moons before we can bring the Ra'ira back," I said. "I think I ought to tell you that I took it on myself to tell Zaddorn the truth about—"

"You *what*?" Ferrathyn interrupted, snapping forward in his chair. The trembling in his arms was more noticeable as he clutched the arm of the chair, and his eyes were flashing. "Rikardon, you had no right—"

I felt myself growing angry. "I had as much right as anyone else who knows," I said, "and far more reason. You forget, I have *faced* the vineh; I know what Zaddorn is up against. And I don't mean to criticize, but I think keeping the truth from him this long was not only unfair, but dangerous to the citizens of Raithskar he is bound to protect."

Thanasset had stood up, and now he came between Ferrathyn and me, holding a raised hand toward each of us.

"There is no reason for anger in this," he said. "Each of you has done what he believed right, has he not?"

The tension lasted a moment longer, then Ferrathyn took a deep breath and relaxed back into his chair. I realized I was leaning forward, too, and made myself sit back.

"You are right as always, my good friend," Ferrathyn said, reaching out to touch Thanasset's arm. "It seems you were right to begin with, when you urged taking Zaddorn into the confidence of the Council. I would apologize for opposing you, but the issue seems inconsequential now."

"Everything is inconsequential," Thanasset said, "except getting back the Ra'ira." He looked at me. "I hesitate to ask, son—having you and Tarani and the sha'um here these few days has been a memorable joy—but . . ."

"You were gone when I woke," I said. "This is the first chance I've had to tell you—we have decided to start the journey back to Eddarta tomorrow."

Thanasset's expression flickered between relief and sadness.

"Milda will be upset," he said. "She spends hours with those cubs." He sat down. "You will all be missed."

"Are you taking the young sha'um with you?" Ferrathyn asked, surprised. "Will that not slow your journey?"

"Better a slow journey than none at all," I said. "Neither of the sha'um would go without the cubs." I leaned over and slapped Thanasset's knee lightly. "I know for a fact that Milda hasn't been out there playing with the cubs all alone," I said. "They love you both, you know. They will miss you."

"I expect you will want an early start," Ferrathyn said, and stood up. I felt glad to see that he did move easily now. Standing, he was barely taller than my head while I was sitting. "I shall not keep you longer."

Thanasset was up again, protesting. "But it is your first visit in so long," he said. "Stay a while, and talk."

"About what?" the old man asked, raising an eyebrow. "The vineh? The Ra'ira? They are the only things worth discussing these days, old friend, and I for one hear enough about them both during the Council meetings." He turned to me, and pressed my shoulder. "I suspect that telling Zaddorn the truth about the Ra'ira belongs on the long list of good things you have done for our city, Rikardon. I apologize for my outburst. I will inform the Council of his knowledge tomorrow and I—um—"

"I'm sure Zaddorn understands why he wasn't told at the beginning," I said.

The old man smiled. "Thank you for trying," he said, "but I see no way out of it. I shall have to apologize to Zaddorn." His eyes twinkled. "I find it hard to predict whether I shall choke on the words, or Zaddorn will die of shock. If your mission were not so urgent, I would invite you to stay and watch."

After Ferrathyn left, Thanasset and I returned to the sitting room and our glasses of barut.

"Zaddorn told me that Ferrathyn had changed," I said. "I

see it, too—he looks older, and that flash of anger was unlike him."

"The crisis has put him under great strain," Thanasset said. "And Zaddorn has not helped the situation. He knew the story about vineh illness was a lie the moment he heard it, and he has been pressing Council members at every opportunity for the truth."

"Challenging Ferrathyn's leadership," I said, "just when he felt it had to be strongest, and just when the theft of the Ra'ira had weakened it. Keeping Zaddorn ignorant probably has been a symbol to Ferrathyn, a confirmation of his position as Chief Supervisor. I pulled that symbol away from him by telling Zaddorn the truth." I shook my head. "No wonder he blew up at me. Apologize for me, the next time you see him, will you?"

"I will not," Thanasset said. "You were right. Even Ferrathyn saw that, as soon as he calmed down. Not only have you given Zaddorn help in the defense of the city, but you have, I hope, put that symbol to rest, so that Zaddorn and the Council can begin to work together again."

"What is the Council doing, now that the duty of watching the vineh with the Ra'ira is nonexistent?" I asked.

Thanasset laughed bitterly. "We are paying the price of luxury," he said. "Organizing work crews to do the cleaning and repairing the vineh used to do. Spending hours each day answering the complaints of people who are impatient with dirty streets, outraged by the idea of cleaning out their own bath filters, or afraid for their safety. Trying to teach people the value of their own labor."

He sighed.

"It would be a thousand times easier with the Ra'ira," he said. "I believe I understand how sorely the Kings were tempted."

The look of shock on my face brought a real laugh from him.

"I am joking," he assured me. "The Council has reached unanimous agreement: When the Ra'ira is returned, the vineh will be guided westward, to an area where other vineh colonies are located. Then the Ra'ira will be destroyed."

"How?" I asked.

"How? Smashed, I suppose. Why do you ask?"

"Because Serkajon threw it into the rakor forge, and it wasn't harmed," I said.

Thanasset gaped at me. We had talked of the time I had spent in the All-Mind, and of what I had learned from the lifememories of Zanek, the first King, and Serkajon, the Sharith Captain who had brought about the end of the Kingdom. Somehow, the detail of Serkajon, while Zanek was Visiting in his body, trying and failing to destroy the blue gemstone, had been omitted.

After a moment, Thanasset threw off his surprise. "A way will be found," he assured me grimly. "The Council failed its charge by using the monstrous thing. The only way to make up for that is to destroy it. Just bring it here," he said. "We will find a way to insure it will never be used again."

In Ricardo's world, it would have been a tearful farewell. As it was, Milda shifted unpredictably from looking calm and brave to a tearless, desperate sobbing that was heartbreaking to hear. She smiled as she handed me the travel bags she had packed, and sobbed when she hugged me. Tarani hugged her, and they both broke down. Thanasset and I were quieter, but no less emotional than the women. He pounded my back and held me fiercely when I hugged him good-bye. The straight, firm line of his mouth softened and trembled when he bent to caress the cubs one more time.

Thanasset, Keeshah, and I waited beside the double gate for the women to finish their farewells.

"Your garden is ruined," I said, waving toward the small hill that had been green and flowery only a few days ago, but was trampled and scarred now.

"In the best possible cause," he said. "I shall take great pleasure in rebuilding it with a large, a very large, open space around the sha'um house."

I laughed and slapped his back.

"You're sure you have enough coin?" he asked.

"Plenty," I assured him.

For some time, I had been wearing a belt with commemorative gold coins sewn inside it. I had changed two of the coins for smaller denominations which were easier to spend, and had traded the rest for less distinctive gold coins

57

of the same value—which were now resewn inside the same belt.

Tarani broke away from Milda, who knelt to embrace the cubs as they ran up to her. Tarani and Yayshah joined us beside the gate. The girl extended her hand toward Thanasset. "You and Milda have been most gracious," she said.

As he had done when he greeted her, Thanasset took her hand, lifted it, and kissed the palm. "You are a part of us now, Tarani," he said. "You leave behind an emptiness that we will mourn until you return."

"I—" she began, but words failed her. The brief awkwardness ended when he opened his arms and she flew into them to hug him.

There seemed to be no more reason to delay. Keeshah's mind was pushing at me to get going. Yayshah was nudging Tarani from behind, betraying her eagerness to get out of the city. The cubs were alert and curious, not really comprehending what was happening, but ready for the adventure it promised.

Beyond the gate, we could hear people moving about and talking quietly. "Word has spread of your leaving," Thanasset said. "The people do not know of your mission, but your very presence here has offered them a target for their restless interest, a distraction from the danger. Many will be waiting to watch you leave. Do you see? It is an *event* for them."

"Yes, I see," I said, then turned to Tarani. "Ask Yayshah if you may ride."

"She is willing, I know," the girl answered. "But did you not tell me that tradition demands walking within the city?" She paused, looking from me to Thanasset, then she smiled her understanding. "I see too," she said. "The distraction of the 'event' outweighs tradition in this case."

Keeshah, I will ride, I told the big cat.

He registered surprise, but crouched down to let me straddle his back. For now, I left the travel packs slung by their joining rope over my shoulder, and sat up straight. As Keeshah stood up, I could see over the fence. A crowd had indeed gathered, and a murmur traveled quickly down the street as the nearest people saw my head and shoulders appear above the fence.

Yayshah crouched and Tarani mounted much more easily than had been possible when Yayshah had been hugely pregnant. Tarani adjusted her travel bag rope on her shoulder as Yayshah surged to her feet; she nodded. Thanasset opened the gate, and waved at me as Keeshah led the procession into and down the street, through a city packed with cheering people.

The cubs walked between their parents, their energy and curiosity making them zigzag back and forth in the clear lane between lines of people. When the kittens got near the edge of the crowd, a curious twitch occurred in the sea of heads, as some people lunged forward to touch the kittens and an equal number flinched back in fear of the consequences.

Stay in line, I told the cubs, with little hope of obedience. Koshah and Yayshah were frisky, getting more excited by the minute. But they made an effort to comply, and kept their zigzag pattern closer to the center of the lane. *Thanks,* I told them. *We'll have the chance to run soon, I promise.*

The crowd made me nervous, and that made Keeshah edgy, and his nervousness compounded mine. Yet we gave Thanasset the show he asked for, the sha'um walking with their stately grace up to and through the huge open gate marking the entrance to Raithskar.

Shouts of good will and joy followed us through the gate. Raithskarians knew very little about the present-day society that had grown from the Sharith, the cat-mounted army which had served the Kings. But every Gandalaran knew that only males left the Valley of the Sha'um, and only men could bond with and ride them.

I felt no compunction about accepting the attention of the crowds. Tarani and Yayshah and the cubs were exactly what Thanasset wanted. They were an historical event in themselves.

8

The crowd followed us for a way outside the city, but stopped when the man in the gray baldric waved them back. The color of his baldric marked him as part of the Peace and Security Force of Raithskar. He was one of several sentries who ringed the city. All of them were armed with swords, daggers, and hollow-bone whistles.

He waved us to a stop, and I slid off of Keeshah's back to speak with him. He greeted me and nodded to Tarani, then spoke quietly. He looked young. I could tell he was nervous.

"The Chief told me you would be leaving this way," the man said. "He asked me to wish you a safe journey, and report what we know of vineh groups."

"Did he warn you the sha'um might stir up another vineh incident?"

The young officer swallowed and nodded.

"We'll try to keep that from happening," I told him, "by avoiding the known groups. Where are they?"

We were still on the road. The young man pulled out his dagger and used the point to draw a sketch of the city. A nearly straight line served as the Great Wall. He talked and pointed. Most of the vineh were on the western side of the city.

"We were returning from the west when they attacked before," I said, looking at the diagram. "We're headed east now; it looks as if we can get away without much trouble. Even if the vineh decide to come after us, the big groups couldn't reach us in time."

I stood up and thanked the officer.

Yoshah, I called the female cub to me. She trotted up, nipped insincerely at my boot, and looked at the young man curiously, drawing a smile from him. I led the cub over to Yayshah, and Tarani leaned forward to hear me.

"There are small groups scattered to the east of the city," I said. "The best thing seems to me to be an all-out run to get out of range as quickly as possible. The cubs can't keep up yet—do you think Yayshah will tolerate carrying Yoshah?"

"I shall ask," Tarani said, closed her eyes for a moment, then nodded. "The question is, will Yoshah put up with it?"

"My turn," I said, and knelt beside the pale-furred kitten.

She stood just higher than knee level. She had looked stubby and awkward at birth, but she was already gaining length to her body so that the thick legs and paws looked more in proportion. As I stroked down the fluffy fur, the darker markings, resembling her mother's brindling, appeared more clearly.

I have to ask you a favor, my girl, I said. *I know you want to run on your own, but it isn't safe yet. Will you lie very still on Yayshah's back until it's safe to get down?*

She rubbed the side of her face against my arm, turning her ear back and twitching it right again.

Neither of the cubs had yet tried to talk to me in words. I could feel Yoshah struggling to say something, and I reached out to listen, trying to get the meaning without needing the words. When it hit me, I barely kept myself from laughing aloud.

Koshah will ride Keeshah, I assured the female cub. *If he refuses, then we will all walk. Okay?*

She agreed readily then, and let me gather her up with my arms around her chest and under her tail—which snapped back and forth. I stood up carefully, and tried to maneuver so the flipping tail wouldn't hit Yayshah in the face.

It's a good thing we're doing this today, I thought. The way they're growing, they might be too heavy to lift tomorrow.

61

"She agreed?" Tarani asked doubtfully.

"The only problem was a touch of jealousy," I explained.

Tarani reached down to help, and we draped Yoshah across her mother's shoulders. Her head was up and she peered around curiously, but for the moment the kitten was doing as she had promised—lying still. Tarani slid her hips toward the big cat's, pulled the kitten toward her, and lay forward over the cub's body. She nodded to me.

"It will work if she stays still," she said.

All right, Yoshah?

She found some words. *Yes. Go?*

In just a minute, I promised.

Something hit my leg—once, twice—as another voice hit my mind.

Memememememe, it called.

I knelt beside the male cub and petted him while I explained what we had to do. He didn't care about the danger; he only wanted what his sister had been given, the privilege of riding a parent.

Sometimes, I thought, as I struggled to lift the slightly heavier male, *jealousy is a useful thing.*

I asked Keeshah to crouch, and I straddled him carefully. Koshah was still, but trembling with excitement. His raspy tongue lashed out and caught my ear, making me nearly drop him. I guided his movements through our link, and got him settled on Keeshah's back. The big sha'um twisted his head around to stare at me, and the mood in his mind was one of exaggerated patience.

All right, Keeshah, I told him. *We're nearly ready.*

Keeshah surged to his feet. I moved back and settled Koshah into position under my torso, and gripped Keeshah's shoulders. I checked Tarani again, where she lay across the hind legs and twitching tail of Yoshah, and she nodded.

East, I said. *Run.*

Tarani must have given the same message to Yayshah, for the two sha'um leaped forward at the same instant. I felt a double "whoop" of joy from the two kittens, and Koshah's body shifted a bit as he clenched himself around Keeshah.

Tell cub no claws, Keeshah complained.

I passed the word to both cubs, and then turned my attention to riding.

A rider doesn't ride *on* his sha'um; he rides *with* his sha'um, distributing his own weight as evenly as possible along the cat's spine. He has to cling tightly enough to keep from bouncing, but keep his body flexible enough to flow with the stretch-and-close movement of the leg action, and the up-and-down effect on the cat's back.

The effort becomes automatic with practice. The rider learns the sha'um's rhythms, and his muscles accommodate the cat's patterns. The sha'um can alert the man to any discomfort through their mindlink, so they develop a riding style that is comfortable for both of them.

Adding a second rider—or a hundred pounds of sha'um cub—changes the combination and defeats that natural, automatic style. We ran for nearly an hour, carrying the cubs, and it was hard work. I judged we were twenty miles or more east of Raithskar when the cubs began to get restless. I called us to a halt. Keeshah and Yayshah crouched low, and Tarani and I let the cubs scramble off their parents. As soon as Tarani stepped away from Yayshah, she flopped over on her side and lay there, panting. Keeshah, accustomed for some time to carrying two people, was barely breathing hard. He kept his crouch and watched the cubs sniffing and prowling through the underbrush.

"I was about to ask to stop," Tarani said. "It was her first run in so long." Her face glowed as she looked at the darkly marked female. "It was hard for her, Rikardon, but she loved it. Not just the run. Running while I was with her. She loved it."

I heard the awe in Tarani's voice, and I sympathized. Apart from any emotional motives, there were sound, logical reasons why a person might want to bond to a sha'um: the defensive strength of the huge cat, faster travel time. There seemed to be no logical advantage to the sha'um in the deal. A sha'um left his home and put the quality of his life—if not his very existence—in the hands of a weak and confused creature, and he seemed to do it solely for the sake of companionship with his bonded friend.

Yayshah was an exception. Before she had left the Valley, she had been promised that she would continue to have the protection of her lifemate, Keeshah, as well as our company. Yet she had made it clear that Tarani, not Keeshah, was the reason she made the choice to leave.

I had learned that the sha'um did get something from their association with people—they shared new sensory experience, and their own native intelligence was stimulated by the need to communicate through the mindlink. But that was a long-term effect, unknown to the sha'um (if they ever realized it) until long after they made their choice.

It's hard for a rational mind to accept an act of love with no gain motive at its base. Being on the receiving end of a sha'um bond is humbling and exalting, and a little frightening—for if you accept that a sha'um is with you by his own choice, you must also accept that he may choose to leave at any time. The end result is that you return his loyalty and love as truly and completely as you can—not because you fear he will leave, but because you admire his innate nobility and want to emulate it.

"I think we're well past the danger from the vineh," I said. "I saw only five groups. Did you spot any others?"

She shook her head. "They seemed to take little notice of us, other than to move away if they were close," she added. "We might have walked in safety—though I agree that the speed of our departure was a wise precaution."

"There were young animals in those groups, and the largest one I saw had only twelve individuals. They seemed to be just minding their own business, but it's hard to tell how they would have reacted if the sha'um had been around longer."

I stretched my arms above my head.

"In any case, I think we've left the vineh danger behind. From here on out, we'll match our pace to what the cubs can manage comfortably. There should be enough wild game in the Morkadahl foothills for Yayshah and Keeshah to have ample opportunity to take the cubs hunting along the way." I brought my arms down, and put one around her shoulders to hug her briefly. "I guess I *was* getting impatient, without realizing it," I admitted. "It feels really good to be moving again."

9

The Morkadahls are a high range of mountains that slash southward from the Great Wall to subdivide the western half of Gandalara. Behind Raithskar, the Great Wall does, indeed, resemble a wall—a sheer escarpment vanishing into the cloud cover above. Gandalarans named the entire northern border of their world the Great Wall, even though the escarpment quickly became more gentle, but still impassable, slopes that seemed indistinguishable from the mountains in the Morkadahls or the Korchis.

It was difficult to believe that the Kapiral Desert and the slopes of the Morkadahls were part of the same environment. It was not difficult to understand the value of water in this world, or why Gandalarans had evolved as water savers who did not sweat at all or weep unnecessarily. The key to the tremendous landscape difference was the presence of water.

Rivers of fresh, cool water descended from the mountains in varied styles of waterfall, from the nearly vertical, thundering Sharkel Falls in Raithskar to the Tashal, whose many widespread branches cascaded and flowed down the River Wall around Eddarta. Where there was a visible and usable water source, there was also a city or a town.

There were some foothills in Gandalara that were as arid and scratchy as the deserts themselves. More often, however, the mountains seemed to soak moisture from the cloud cover. The Morkadahl foothills were fertile and busy with life. To the east, they sheltered a unique triangle of

65

what I thought of as "true forest"—tall trees, rich under-growth, a darkish and sheltered place that was the exclusive territory of the sha'um.

We followed the western slopes of the Morkadahls, angling northward and then traveling south. There were two major settlements along the way: Alkhum, which footed the painfully high Khumbar Pass across the Mor-kadahls into the Valley of the Sha'um; and Omergol, a city built almost exclusively of the beautiful green marble its people quarried for export.

We stopped at the cities, Tarani and I leaving the sha'um briefly to indulge in a bath and a hot meal, and to sleep on a fluffy pallet instead of the ground. We bought more "trail" food—dried meat and fresh fruits, and flattish, savory bread—and refilled the eight water pouches we carried between us.

In Omergol, we stayed at the Green Sha'um Inn, and I introduced Tarani to Grallen, the inn's owner and a man I considered my friend. He greeted Tarani with a quiet word and a smile broad enough to display the gap in his lower teeth—the earmark of a rough road to success—and winked at me as he left the table to order our meal. The girl who had drawn such a crowd when I had been here last—in the company of Thymas, the son of the leader of the Sharith—performed that night, as well. Tarani was as fascinated as we had been by the music that issued from the flutelike instrument, guided by the skill of the player.

The following morning, someone knocked on the door of our room just as we were shouldering our "saddlebags" and getting ready to leave. I opened the door, and could not conceal my shock.

"Somil?" I gasped.

The tall, nearly bald, old man smiled, crossed his arms, and leaned on the doorsill.

"I heard you were here, and suspected you would not stay long," he said, nodding at the travel bag suspended from my shoulder. "I would have the answer to at least one of your mysteries, my friend: did you find Kä?"

Behind me, Tarani grabbed the laminated-wood door and pulled it open wider.

"It is the way of the Record to serve," she said, sounding

as if she were quoting a maxim, "not to question." The words were severe, but her tone was curious.

Somil pulled himself upright and inclined his head toward the girl. His supraorbital ridge arched slightly, giving him a built-in arrogant look which he reinforced with arrogant behavior. His eyes twinkled as he looked at Tarani.

"Have you not heard, Tarani, that Somil is a renegade Recorder, who regularly betrays tradition?"

Tarani showed no surprise that Somil knew her name, but smiled with her own look of mischief. "I have heard much worse things of the notorious Somil," she said, then grew serious. "The only source I trust completely," she said, touching my shoulder lightly, "speaks highly of your skill and discretion." She stepped forward; I edged aside to give her room in the doorway. Tarani extended both of her hands and bowed. "I am honored to meet you, Recorder."

Somil grasped her hands and returned the bow. "And I you, Recorder," he echoed.

"The answer to your question," I said, "is yes. But—" He raised a hand and waved it.

"Say no more," he urged me. "I will not hold you from your journey to hear the tale, though I would listen eagerly. To know that you had some profit from our seeking is enough for now."

He stood away from the doorway and invited us through it with a gesture. Tarani picked up her travel bags, and the three of us walked downstairs. At the door of the inn, Somil spoke again.

"I trust you realize," he said to me, "that you have done something I thought impossible—you have made me more interested in the events of the present than in those of the past. It would be cruel to leave that interest, once stirred, unsatisfied."

"If you're asking us to come back and tell you the whole story someday, that's a promise," I said. "When it will be—"

Again, he waved his hand. "Before my death is all I ask," he said. He bowed to Tarani again, wished us a fair journey, and walked away without looking back.

Tarani and I turned to move down the broad, stepped avenue leading through the center of Omergol.

"He knew me through his contact with you while you

67

were seeking," she said. "I would give a great deal to know what he saw of me in your mind."

I reached for her hand and twined my fingers between hers. "What he saw, you know. Haven't we agreed to be honest with one another from now on?"

Outside of Omergol, we rejoined the sha'um, who were snoozing in an "orchard"—a cultivated field of dakathrenil trees. On the wild hillsides, the trees curled and twisted close to the ground, each tree looking more like a waist-high bush. Where the trees crowded together, younger ones had to reach higher for the light. We had seen clumps of dakathrenil yards long and several tiers high, rising taller than a man's head. The trees had needle-shaped leaves, bore a nutlike fruit, and provided shelter and food to an astounding variety of small animals.

Gandalarans cultivated the dakathrenil to grow straighter and taller. The trees were short-lived, grew fast, and reproduced plentifully. Their fruit was a major crop, but the real profit to a farmer was in the wood of the dead trees. Converting the zigzag trunks into functional articles was a task that involved many skills and supported many trades: cutting and smoothing small pieces from the trunks, laminating the largest pieces to form tools or doors or furniture, using the smaller pieces in artful decoration.

Koshah, the male cub, was the first to wake as we approached. He yawned, laying his ears back and stretching his front legs, one at a time, out in front of him. Then he dug his claws into the ground and dragged his body forward and up, stretching out his hind legs and arching the tail, half as long as his torso, which was never still while he was awake.

We had made it a leisurely trip, taking many breaks for naps and hunting lessons for the sha'um, and covering about the same distance each day that a man could walk. Still, barely two weeks had passed since we had left Raithskar, and the development of the cubs during that time had been phenomenal. Yayshah had begun the weaning process by pre-chewing meat from Keeshah's kills, and the cubs' teeth—including the two upper tusks characteristic of most Gandalaran mammals, but especially prominent in the sha'um—were fully visible and usable now. The

68

cubs had begun to lose the long, fluffy, silver-tipped fur that had overlaid and masked their markings, and were emerging as miniatures of their parents.

I could see their development in less visible ways. Their mindvoices were changing, taking on weight and confidence, communicating more deliberately and clearly. I had made a real effort to stay out of the way, so to speak, while they were being taught to be sha'um—but they had not allowed it. Like children looking over their shoulders to assure themselves they had an audience, they had drawn my awareness with them into the process of watching, scenting, waiting, stalking.

I had learned something from those lessons. The first time the cubs had watched Yayshah bring down a wild glith, their minds had erupted and carried me, breathless, into a maelstrom of fierce, predatory excitement. Tarani and I had been strolling; I had wrenched myself away to awaken flat on the ground, with Tarani kneeling beside me, nearly panicked by my sudden collapse.

Raw power ran through the minds of the cubs, a product of the incautious enthusiasm of youth. While I treasured their desire to share their every experience with me, I had learned to be prepared to disengage from the more intense experiences.

The problem had changed as Koshah and Yoshah had become more verbal and less . . . primal. While they had been two distinct individuals from the start, I had thought of them together as "the cubs." They diverged rapidly into separate, equally demanding presences. Each cub was constantly discovering something new and trying to tell me about it. I wanted to encourage their enthusiasm for talking, so I ruthlessly suppressed my occasional—and inevitable—"What is it *now*?" attitude and responded with interest and approval. The practice was teaching me to balance the three warm presences and fine-tune my end of the communication, so that I could speak to any one of the sha'um directly and privately.

Koshah trotted over to greet us, squeezing himself between Tarani and me so that he could rub against both of us. When he had passed through, Tarani knelt. The male cub went up to her, rubbed his cheek against hers, and let his chin rest on her shoulder while her hands stroked his head and the longer neckfur that could lift into a mane. Koshah closed his eyes and enjoyed it, as only a cat can enjoy being petted. Tarani smiled softly and enjoyed it, too.

Soon all the sha'um were awake. Yoshah demanded the same kind of treatment from me, and I obliged until Keeshah said: *Go soon?*

10

We traveled south from Omergol and around the tip of the range, marked by a mountain that shot up unexpected from the foothills: Mount Kadahl. As had been true throughout the trip, more time was spent in hunting than in moving. The adult sha'um could store food (and water, for that matter) for long periods. They hunted to teach and feed the cubs, who were *never* not hungry. What they ate seemed to turn directly into growth. They had added inches in length and height since Raithskar, and had begun to look so scrawny that Tarani and I discussed the possibility that the travel was harming them, and slowed the pace even further.

Our fears were unfounded. During the seven days between Omergol and Thagorn, the up-and-out growth process gave way to a thickening of muscle. By the time we sighted the Sharith scout, each cub was about the size of a full-grown tiger, and their birthfur was almost entirely gone.

Yoshah, whose sense of smell seemed keener than the others', was the first to lift her head alertly. The announcement of the newcomer was a growly noise in her throat. To me she said: *Strange sha'um.* The ruff of gray fur around her neck fluffed out, and her tail stopped its miscellaneous movement, only the tip twitching from side to side.

It is a friend, I said to Yoshah, broadening the message to include Koshah, as well. The cubs heard me, but waited tensely for the newcomer to appear.

They were going to be disappointed.

"As we agreed?" I said to Tarani. She nodded.

Stay here, I told the cubs, and to Keeshah I said: *Let's go meet the Rider.*

Keeshah moved out, only to be halted by three impatient sha'um voices—two, as I could tell, wanting to go along, and one trying to stop them. Keeshah turned back and added his command to Yayshah's, and I reached with my mind to soothe the cubs' indignation at being left behind. Tarani rode Yayshah skillfully as the sha'um lunged forward and used her nose to try to force Koshah away from us. The male cub snarled and twisted quickly, and brought a paw up (claws sheathed) to knock his mother's head out of the way. For that, he got a swat against his side that sent him tumbling.

Keeshah jumped into the act. He brought his head down against his daughter's side and half-threw her back toward Yayshah. She got up and stalked forward, her ears flattened, and thought better of it when Keeshah bared his teeth and crouched.

Want to go, Koshah told me, still trying to edge around Yayshah to get to us.

Stay here, I repeated to both cubs. *We'll be back in a little while.*

Other sha'um close, Keeshah said, and the information was confirmed by the sounds of movement through the brush. I caught a glimpse of the crown of a hat, above a clump of wild dakathrenil.

"Hello the sentry," I called. "Please stay where you are; I will join you shortly."

The hat stopped and rose, revealing first the round, flat brim and then the eyes of the face underneath it.

"As you wish, Captain," the man answered. The voice was unfamiliar.

You're going to stay put, right? I asked the cubs, and received a grudging agreement. Keeshah whirled and launched himself in a long, loping stride around the tree tangle. In seconds we were face to face with the Sharith Rider.

"Welcome to Thagorn, Captain," the man said formally. "I am Innis, and this is Wortel." He drew his hand along the left jaw of the sha'um he was riding.

We had met before, of course. I had met each of the Riders on the occasion when Dharak had declared me Captain, the first in Gandalaran history since Serkajon had left Kingdom and Sharith in order to remove the power of the Ra'ira from the Kings. But there were nearly a hundred Riders. I appreciated the man's reintroducing himself and his sha'um, and repaid the gesture by performing the formal introduction for Keeshah.

The Rider was young, barely in his twenties. The roving patrol guarding Thagorn was usually the assignment of the older Riders. Seeing so young a man on this duty brought remembrance and concern sharply into focus.

"How many sha'um, Innis?" I asked urgently.

He hesitated, as if he would have suggested I wait and ask Thymas, but he must have read the need for answers in my face.

"Twelve more since you and the lady Tarani left, Captain," the man said. "All of them in the first seven-day; none since then."

I forced my shoulder to relax and sighed. *Twelve more*, I thought. *That brings the total to thirty-four sha'um who returned to the Valley early, solely because Yayshah came along and reminded them they were males. And roughly a seventh of the sha'um were already in the Valley, responding to the natural mating cycle.* I felt my chest tighten with grief and sympathy for the Riders whose sha'um had broken contact and reverted to their animal state. I had been through that myself, recently—it was no picnic. It felt as if a part of your brain had been surgically removed. You couldn't think or see or feel. You were not complete. You were alone.

"Uh, sir?" Innis prompted hesitantly.

"Yes, Innis," I said, coming back out of my reverie. "I was just thinking—nearly half of the Riders must be suffering."

"Sir, Lieutenant Thymas has made it clear that you are not to blame for the situation. His instructions to the sentries are always the same—to offer you welcome and the hospitality of Thagorn. And I"—he cleared his throat and sat up a little straighter, "I am proud to do so, sir."

"Thank you," I said, more unnerved than I let on. Even

73

under the stress of the early departure of his sha'um for the Valley, Dharak had taken the trouble to write the appointment for his son. "Lieutenant Thymas," I thought.

"Tell me one more thing, Innis—how is Dharak?"

The man's face told me all I needed to know, and I did not wait for him to say it out loud.

"Please wait here for a moment," I said.

"My instructions, sir," Innis said, as Keeshah turned back in the direction from which we had appeared, "are to offer welcome to the lady Tarani, as well."

"Tarani joins with me in wishing no further disruption to the Sharith, and has chosen not to enter Thagorn," I told him, looking back over my shoulder. "But I will convey your welcome, Innis. It will please her greatly."

When we returned to the group of sha'um (the cubs were pacing about, pouting in mind and mannerism, but silent), I told Tarani what Innis had said. As I had expected, she was very moved. We had left Thagorn at my insistence while Yayshah had been largely and clumsily pregnant, and unpredictably near to delivering the cubs. Tarani, both because she rationally and wholly cared for the female, and because she was mindlinked and a little too closely in touch with Yayshah's feelings, had resisted that decision.

After the cubs were born, and Tarani had learned more control of the recently established mindlink, she had been in a unique position to appreciate the magnitude of Yayshah's effect on the Sharith. She now shared the same kind of bond that had been suddenly and unexpectedly removed from the Riders of the missing sha'um. And she had witnessed and suffered from my breakdown when Keeshah had left me.

The respect of the Sharith was of immense importance to her, yet she would have accepted their hatred of Yayshah— and herself—without apology. It was a bonus for her that they seemed to understand, as we did, that what had happened was unfortunate but not intentional.

I invited her to ride with me into Thagorn, but she shook her head. "Let us do as we agreed, and one of us stay with the family at all times, to warn away the other sentries. I would not have another Rider suffer the loss of his sha'um."

So I rode alone beside Innis into Thagorn, through the

gates of a wall stretching like a dam across a deep narrow opening, closing in a large and verdant valley. On our last visit to the city of the Sharith, Tarani and I had been greeted with a great deal of ceremony. This time, no one had warning of our arrival, so that Innis and I rode in like two ordinary Riders returning from patrol duty.

That lasted as long as it took for the guards on the wall to recognize me. Then my name was shouted and passed along the length of the valley, and people came running from all directions. At the midpoint of the valley, it was bisected by a strong river. Just this side of the river stood a large, white stone house—the home of the Lieutenant. I headed in that direction, slowing Keeshah to a walk, and pausing frequently to greet people I recognized.

This crowd was unlike the one in Raithskar. For one thing, they kept their distance, shouting and waving. For another, there was a subdued quality, even to the laughter, and I knew that the sight of me reminded them of the grounded Riders. Yet what Innis had implied was true: There was no accusation here, only great curiosity about the fate of the woman who had broken the ageless men-only tradition of the Riders and the female sha'um who had broken instinct to bear her cubs outside the Valley.

In the distance, near the white house, I saw a figure come out the front door, mount a crouching sha'um, and ride toward us. The crowd parted to let Thymas pass; he rode up beside me and laid his right hand on my right shoulder. I returned the salute and, mindful of the crowd, held back the questions that tumbled into my head.

How long have we been gone? I wondered. *Two months? Three? Thymas has aged five years in that time.*

I turned partly away from Thymas and spoke to the group of people, most of whom were non-Riders who had been at work at the many tasks necessary to support a settlement of the size of Thagorn.

"Your greeting honors me," I said. "Tarani and Yayshah are well, and two cubs have joined us." A clamor rose at that, the words obscured by the sheer noise of the outburst. The meaning was clear; these people whose lives were so thoroughly intertwined with sha'um, wanted desperately to see the cubs.

75

Thymas raised his hand, and quiet settled in quickly.

"Innis, you know the location of the Lady Tarani?"

"Yes, sir."

"Then kindly return to her. When Wortel scents the female, dismount and send him upwind, and approach Tarani on foot. Give her my greeting, and ask if she and the sha'um will consent to be settled in the clearing prepared for them."

The Rider turned his sha'um and rode back through the gates. Thymas addressed the crowd.

"The Captain and I will consider the possibility of allowing Sharith to visit Yayshah and her cubs in small groups, but if it can be permitted, such visits will not begin until tomorrow. We must give Rikardon and Tarani a night's rest, at least."

The crowd began to dissipate. Thymas turned Ronar, his sha'um, and rode beside me toward the white house.

"What is this 'clearing?'" I asked him.

"Just that," he said, "a clearing . . . with a house. It is some distance from Thagorn, but sheltered in the hills, and—"

"And downwind," I interrupted, looking at him in surprise. "Thymas, you built a house for us?"

We stopped our sha'um and faced each other. There was more sincerity than I could bear in the boy's voice as he said, "Tarani has proven herself to be Sharith, and you are our Captain. You spared us the shame of asking you to leave us, and I swore that necessity would not arise again. That house may not be *in* Thagorn, but it is *of* the Sharith. It will serve as your—and Tarani's—home, or as a temporary shelter for your visits. That is your choice; the house is yours, whenever it is needed."

I was at a loss for words. I urged Keeshah on and we rode in silence, to dismount in front of the Lieutenant's house. Shola came out, wiping her hands on her apron. She hesitated for an awkward moment, then impulsively hugged me. I returned the hug, and put an arm around Thymas as we went into the house.

Dharak was in the sitting room, arranged in an armchair, silent and motionless, staring out the window.

11

᾽ A shudder of tension ran through me and the two people I was touching. Shola said awkwardly, "It is the luncheon hour, Captain, and we were preparing to eat. You will join us, of course?" She was a chunky, hearty woman who could be beautiful when she wished. She was looking up at me with an air of *not* looking at her husband, and the rounded cheeks seemed hollow, the skin of her arms loose, the goldish headfur thinning noticeably.

"It has never lasted this long before, has it, Shola?" I asked her quietly.

She closed her eyes and took a breath. "It will be this way," she said shakily, "until Doran returns. I am sure of it."

I squeezed her shoulder. "Would I pass up one of your meals, Shola? Please go on ahead; Thymas and I will be there in just a moment."

She left us, the boy and I, looking at the palefurred man who had led the Sharith for most of a long and capable life. We had found him in nearly the identical position when we had returned from Omergol with the note that Dharak had scrawled and sent to us. It had named Thymas as Lieutenant.

"Captain," Thymas said suddenly, stepping away and half-turning his back on me. "Please stay in Thagorn."

It was difficult for him to say that, I thought.

"What's wrong, Lieutenant?" I asked.

The boy whirled. "*That's* wrong," he said. "I don't want to be the Lieutenant, not this way."

"You knew it would happen someday," I said. "You hoped for it, didn't you? How would it be different if Dharak were dead, instead of just . . . missing, as he is?"

The words shocked him, but I knew Thymas. It was like the old story with the jackass and the two-by-four; first you had to get his attention. Thymas was either learning discretion, or was getting to know me, too. He started toward me with anger in his face, but stopped, took a deep breath, and smiled wryly.

"The difference is, I haven't had the training I expected," he said. "Oh, I can assign duty and plan sentry patterns and supervise a work crew. If people have to do things, I can see that they work at it. But I don't know a thing about how to control the way people *feel*. And—Rikardon, you don't know what it is like now. The Riders are all right on the surface, but there's not a one of them who goes to sleep with the assurance that his sha'um will be there in the morning. The others function, they do their work, but all they think about—they don't even talk about it, mind you, for fear it will make things worse—is how things have changed, and how they might change tomorrow."

Thymas lifted his arms and dropped them, in a gesture of futility.

"I can *direct* people," he told me. "I can't *lead* them. I never knew the difference until . . . " He waved a hand in the direction of his father.

"How can my staying be of help?" I asked. "And what did you mean by 'training'? What training have you missed?"

"I was a cub the last time Doral went to the Valley," Thymas said. "My father was shocked and upset for a few days, but he came back to himself. He had to step down from being Lieutenant, of course. Only a Rider can lead the Riders. So he appointed someone to take his place temporarily—it was Bareff, in fact."

Bareff had been one of the first two Sharith I had met, and had become and remained a friend. I felt a surge of pride for him.

"Bareff led the Sharith for that year—but not *alone*, Captain. He did the planning, assigning, and supervising—the same kind of things I can do. But the *authority*, the settling of arguments, the award of punishment, the

. . . the *leadership* continued to be Dharak's in action and responsibility. Bareff worked with him, learned from him."

"Are you saying," I asked, "that if things had happened normally, Dharak would be doing that for you? That you and he would share the position of Lieutenant?"

"I am saying exactly that, Captain," he said, and seemed relieved that I understood.

"And you want me here to fill Dharak's place?" I demanded. "Thymas, you can do this alone."

To my surprise, he nodded. "I know that. I also know that I will do it better, with help. And there is something else I fear."

I waited.

"You were right about this being the wrong season for the sha'um to leave. They will be in the Valley for more than a year." He ran a hand through the thick, startling white headfur he had inherited from his father. "By the time Doral comes back, Rikardon, I might be . . . accustomed to being Lieutenant. It may be hard for me to release that authority—or, rather, to live here happily, once it has been released.

"If you are here during that time, the authority transfer will be from you to Dharak. I feel I could live with that much more easily. Will you stay?"

"I can't, Thymas," I said. "You know why."

The wry smile returned. "You would not begrudge me the power to wish, would you?"

"Absolutely not," I said. "Shall we go have lunch?"

As we walked through the doorway into the dining area, I looked back over my shoulder at the quiet, white-haired man sitting by the window, and felt a thrill of shock.

Dharak was no longer staring out the window. His hands remained limp and unmoving on the arms of the chair, but his head had turned, and his eyes were focused on Thymas's back.

I said nothing to Shola or Thymas about the change I had seen in Dharak. *No use getting their hopes up,* I thought. *But I'm sure the Lieutenant heard that plea for help, and is working as hard as he can to come back—for his son's sake.*

I remembered watching Thymas's face in Eddarta, when he had attacked me under Gharlas's mindcontrol, resisting that control and finally breaking it.

79

Thymas got his physical strength naturally, I thought, *but he got his character strength from his father's example, not his genes. Dharak has made a start—he'll pull out of it in his own time.*

Throughout lunch, I had the pleasant sensation of knowing someone else's happy secret and saving it as a surprise for my friends. After lunch, I called Keeshah and we followed Thymas's directions to the house he had built for us.

South of Thagorn's wall, a narrow trail broke away toward the northwest. It had the look of being well-traveled recently, and the ground bore the tracks of wheels and evil-tempered vleks. Obviously, the trail had been used to haul building materials from Thagorn to the site of the house.

It was a large stone house, set slightly off center in a nearly circular clearing some fifty yards in diameter and, incredibly, beside a small, chattering brook. The rivulet was a ground spring, obviously the surface extension of an underground branch of Thagorn's river, which seemed not to have a name.

Around the house was wild country—some of the wildest I had seen. Fed by the plentiful ground water, dakathrenil twisted everywhere, rising even taller than orchard height. I heard movement in the brush, and the touch of Yoshah's mind, stalking. The sha'um would break their own trails through that growth-choked wilderness, and love every minute of it.

Tarani came out of the house as I rode up and slid down from Keeshah's back. The male sha'um drank from the stream and pushed his way out into the brush, seeking his family.

Tarani lifted her arms. "This is wonderful, is it not? The Rider who directed me here—Innis, I believe his name was—spoke of it proudly. The Sharith seem sure that, enclosed as this place is by higher hills, Yayshah's scent will not reach Thagorn."

"Yes," I agreed, "it is well planned. And, as you might have guessed, it was Thymas's idea."

For a moment her eyes went out of focus, and I recognized the fond look on her face. She and Thymas had been more than friends at one time, and I had finally learned to accept that the closeness that continued between them was based on the fact that they had grown and changed away from a very special relationship, and was not a continuation of that relationship.

"Everyone wants to see the cubs, of course," I said. "Thymas has proposed that a few people at a time might visit here—on foot—to meet them. Will Yayshah allow that?"

Her eyes focused on me briefly, then looked over my shoulder as she spoke to the female sha'um.

"She agrees," Tarani said, sighing. "She loves it here, Rikardon. She is planning a den—has already started shaping it, in fact."

"Let her build it," I said, waving at the house behind Tarani. "After all, we have a home waiting for us now, whenever we need it."

Her smile was sad. "It seems we have many homes," she said, "and none that we can enjoy for very long."

"It won't always be this way, Tarani," I said. "Someday, we'll have time—" My voice trailed off as Tarani raised her hand and shook her head.

"It is this way, for the present," she said, "and we have both accepted it. To dream of a change is to focus beyond a task that has not yet been accomplished, and thus distract us from it."

Her voice was sharp, her manner tense.

"Afraid you'd *like* the quiet life?" I asked.

Her head snapped up, but she bit back what would have been an angry reply when she saw my face. She even smiled.

"I could bear it as easily as you could," she said.

Touché, I thought, and had the odd, unsettling feeling of a man who has just examined his life goal and wondered whose it was. *I could have had the "quiet life" with Illia. Maybe when I turned my back on her, I rejected it for good and all?*

I covered my sudden uncertainty by putting my arm around Tarani and moving toward the open doorway.

"I take it back," I said. "If you're there, life couldn't possibly be quiet."

We stayed for six days. In that time, nearly everyone in Thagorn came for a visit, and the cubs grew sleek from the plentiful game and spoiled by all the attention. Yoshah and Koshah were able to stalk and hunt small game themselves, and were eagerly curious about our visitors. Keeshah and Yayshah took advantage of their break from educating the cubs to sleep a lot.

Yayshah benefited greatly from the long rest. Her darkish fur began to look healthier than it had since she had left the Valley, and the skin of her belly, thinned and stretched by the weight of the cubs during her pregnancy, shrank up and flattened out. Tarani took her out for long runs—always *away* from Thagorn, and with plenty of warning to the Sharith. Woman and sha'um both came back glowing from the exercise and the closeness.

Thymas was at our house on the evening of the sixth day, sharing an after-dinner glass of barut with Tarani and me. We had brought armchairs out of the house, to sit and watch the sha'um while we talked.

Only there were no sha'um to watch; they were out of sight beyond the edge of the clearing. We had only a few minutes before the sun went down and the world went dark, and I already knew—though I had not told Thymas as yet—that this would be our last night in Thagorn.

Thymas ought to have a chance to say goodbye to the cubs, I thought, then called: *Yoshah. Koshah. Come here for a second, please.*

We heard a slight rustling, and a dark-colored head popped out of the brush to our left. The cubs had created a warren of tunnels through the tangled brush, their openings cunningly hidden.

Yoshah stepped out, jumped (I could feel her surprise and flash of anger), and whirled to clout the paw Koshah had used to swat her tail. Koshah lunged out of the brush and tried to tumble her with a rush into her side, but she kept her feet, sidestepping to absorb the shock of his head connecting with her flank. She twisted around and nipped at his shoulder (I felt the pinch, and Koshah's anger).

Here, that's enough of that, I said sternly, a little afraid that the play would blossom into a full-blown fight. *Behave yourselves and come over here to say goodbye to Thymas. We'll be leaving tomorrow.*

That was good enough news to distract the cubs from their quarrel. They loped over to us and pressed their heads under my extended hands, their minds full of questions and excitement.

I turned to my left, to speak to Thymas, and realized belatedly that I had not mentioned the fact that I was mindlinked to the cubs. That he understood it now was patently obvious.

"The female, too?" he asked, after a moment.

Tarani, who was seated to my right, leaned forward to look around me at the boy. "Only I am bonded to Yayshah," she said quietly.

Thymas was in shock, searching for words. "But—is it not too soon for them? Why—how—*three*?"

He did not have to say how unfair it seemed, that I should be mindlinked to three sha'um while so many of his men were now deprived of that so-important connection.

Thymas and Tarani and I had talked frequently in those six days, but our conversation had often been public, and had not seriously included the Ra'ira—past, present, or future—as a topic. Thymas knew we had found the sword, and were on our way to Eddarta to reclaim the jewel. But he had not heard about Raithskar and the situation there.

He learned of it then, as I described the vineh attack and the formation of the link with the two cubs. As it happened, the discussion led right into the topic I had been avoiding all evening. "We have to move on, Thymas. We'll be leaving tomorrow."

The boy stood up, and set his empty glass on a table we had brought out of the house, along with the chairs. Night had come, diffused moonlight providing only a dim gray illumination. Beside the door of the house was an oil lamp; Tarani used a striker to light it, and Thymas's shadow leaped out into the clearing.

"I will tell the people in the morning," he said. "It would be best, I think, if you left quietly. You know that our good wishes go with you."

I stood up too. "If circumstances were different," I began.

"They are not different," he snapped, then softened. "I

see you know me well, Captain. I *would* rather go with you than stay here. But I begin to believe as my father did—*does*. . . . The theft of the Ra'ira has signaled a time of change—perhaps the very change for which the Sharith have remained ready all these generations." He frowned. "Yet we are less ready than ever—our Riders at half-strength, our people demoralized and discouraged."

I pressed his arm. "Eddarta will fall to Tarani bloodlessly, we hope—but in any case through logic, and not by force. By the time the Sharith are needed as a weapon—which I hope will never happen—Thagorn will have recovered fully."

He nodded—a little doubtfully it seemed. "What do you need for the journey?" he asked.

"Food and water," Tarani said, coming up behind me, "we can take from the generous stores you have already provided. What we need from you, Thymas, is a friend's farewell."

She moved around my chair to kiss and embrace the boy. *I should be jealous*, I thought. Instead, I was deeply moved; I stood up and put my arms around both of them, sharing their embrace.

12

We left Thagorn at dawn the next morning. The cubs were cheerful and excited, looking forward to a trip I knew would be exhausting and uncomfortable, but happily ignoring my cynicism. Keeshah was glad to be moving, and Tarani said that Yayshah had shown less reluctance to leave her half-built den than she had expected.

We headed east, and quickly left the valley greenery behind us. In Keeshah's mind was an awareness that the Valley of the Sha'um lay north of us. In my mind was the terrifying memory of crawling along a gravelly slope through a blinding, poisonous smog.

The Well of Darkness, the volcanic depression that continually cloaked itself in its own sooty mantle, also lay north of us. Tarani and I had tried to use it to elude pursuit, and had failed. We had climbed out of the blackness to the rim of the Well to face Obilin's attack—and to be rescued by Keeshah, who had sensed my need and broken free of the layer of instinct entrapping him.

The country between Thagorn and Relenor, the Refreshment House resting at the foot of the Zantil Pass, was not quite desert, nor was it green. The land was rocky and dusty, but fairly rich with the gray-leaved bushes which had adapted to desert existence. The first day's traveling went smoothly. The second day, the ground shivered.

The cubs flattened themselves on the ground, and broadcasted fear so strongly and suddenly that I was caught by surprise. I fastened myself more tightly to Keeshah's back, and screamed at him with my mind to run, and he was far away from the cubs by the time I found my senses again. There was fear in Keeshah's mind, but nothing like the absolute terror the cubs were suffering.

We turned back. Yayshah was half-crouching over the cubs, shielding and comforting them with her body. Tarani was standing beside them.

"Is the Well of Darkness causing this?" Tarani asked. "The . . . volcano?"

"I think so," I said, still trying to catch my breath after the rush of panic I had shared with the cubs.

"Does that mean—will it *erupt*?" Tarani asked worriedly, using the Italian term for a word the Gandalaran language had never needed to develop.

"I doubt it," I said, hoping I was right. "It must be mildly active all the time, to keep replenishing that drift of ashy smoke. It's just getting a little more active, that's all."

I had time to be grateful for Tarani's accessing Antonia's memories so that I could explain things clearly without much effort—because calming the cubs took all the patience and concentration I could muster. The tremor had lasted only a few seconds, and I could detect no further movement, but the cubs took a *lot* of convincing. Finally, they loosened their deathgrips on the rocky ground and nervously followed their parents as we moved on.

Have you felt that before? I asked Keeshah.

Yes, he answered.

While you were in the Valley? I prompted him.

Yes, he said, and I began to breathe more easily. If the tremors had been going on since Keeshah's cubhood in the Valley, then this one was nothing special to worry about.

We reached Relenor toward evening of the second day, and were welcomed with the same friendliness we encountered at every Refreshment House. For reasons I never have understood clearly, the Fa'aldu—desert dwellers who seemed to be able to draw water from out of nowhere, and guarded the secret carefully—had chosen to honor me as if I were a hero. Part of it lay with Balgokh, at the Refreshment House of Yafnaar, who had been the first person to see the revived Markasset. He had helped me, and had been aware of the difference in me. He was another, like Dharak, who seemed to sense imminent change, and he had alerted all the Fa'aldu to provide me (and Tarani) anything we needed.

Tarani and I had the privilege of dining with the Relenor family in the interior court of the Fa'aldu dwelling, rather than in the spartan guest quarters the Fa'aldu maintained for the use of travelers.

It had become a minor tradition that I traded stories for the meals the Fa'aldu so generously shared with me. I told Lussim, the Elder of this Refreshment House, about trying to shelter Yayshah in Thagorn, and the tragedy that resulted. I took the story to Raithskar, to the birth of the cubs, and out into the desert. The family was shaken and awed by the idea of walking through a city so ancient, and the secret of the sword's hiding place was a wonder to them. I had developed a real skill at the artful omission of fact, and managed to avoid any reference to Tarani's true state and the effect of the sword on her two personalities.

They grieved over the loss of the third cub as if one of their own had died, and expressed deep concern over the state of things in Raithskar. I edged around the truth again, and let them believe that taking the sha'um from the city had reduced the danger to the citizens of Raithskar, and that the vineh illness would wear away in time.

They had known Tarani before meeting me, though their friendship had not been extended so completely to her. The announcement that we were going to Eddarta to proclaim her real identity as the rightful High Lord was greeted with amazement and a mixture of dismay and delight—delight at the newest twist of what was taking on the proportions of a romantic saga, and dismay that she was to become a fixture in Eddarta.

The Fa'aldu maintained a neutral position in the affairs of men outside the walls of Refreshment Houses, but they knew a lot about them, and were too normal not to make judgments. On the other side of the world, the Fa'aldu had violated their own tradition to offer succor and help to the slaves who escaped from Eddarta's copper mines. They were unaware that the system they thought foolproof ended in Chizan—in death or a different sort of slavery for the people they "helped."

The Fa'aldu in the Refreshment Houses west of the high

crossings that divided Gandalara did not know of their kindred's activity against Eddarta, but they shared the feeling of disapproval. Eddarta was a weighted society, top-heavy with the Lords' wealth at the expense of the effort of the "common man." And the Fa'aldu had an historical reason for disagreeing with the concepts governing Eddarta. The Refreshment Houses were the product of a generous King who had set up a fair system by which everyone could share the skill of the Fa'aldu, and they would be well compensated for their art. Eddarta was the product of the last King, a selfish King, who had fled from Kä and rebuilt his power in the form of an economic autocracy.

By Fa'aldu reasoning, there was nothing good about the Lords. To find out that Tarani, whom they respected and liked, was a Lord by birth was something of a shock.

"And when you rule Eddarta," Lussim asked quietly of Tarani, "what will you do?"

"The present High Lord, my natural brother Indomel," Tarani said, "has the Ra'ira." The group gasped. That the Ra'ira had been stolen from Raithskar was common knowledge; Lussim and his people knew that I had been pursuing the thief on the last occasion I had stopped here. Obviously, they were not blind to the history of the stone, or the possible significance of its being in the hands of a descendant of the Kings.

"I shall send the Ra'ira back to Raithskar, where it belongs," she said. "And I shall begin a change in Eddarta, away from the rule of whim and toward fair treatment. I am not so much a fool to think I shall change the attitude of the Lords completely and immediately, but I can make a beginning. That," she said, "is my only purpose in claiming my rightful place."

The Fa'aldu around the dinner table broke out into a bustling noise of approval, while I, seated directly across from Tarani, stared at her in open-mouthed shock. She stared at the empty plate in front of her and refused to meet my eyes, and I recovered my composure.

Later, in our room—a guest room in the Fa'aldu quarters, rather than in the transients' cubicles—I repeated her words that had alarmed me at the dinner table. "'Send the Ra'ira back to Raithskar?'"

She sat down on the huge salt block that, covered with a pallet, served as a double bed. "Rikardon, please understand—I feel confused and uncertain. Until I was asked the question, until I spoke the words, I had not realized that I expect to—to stay in Eddarta for a time. Shall I win the acclaim of the Lords, deliver them and all of Eddarta from Indomel's crafty selfishness, only to seize the Ra'ira and abandon them again? Would not that be as selfish an act as anything Indomel might do?" She looked up at me, her eyes troubled. "When the Ra'ira is ours, and any possible danger from Indomel is prevented, will that not satisfy the task?"

"And what about the vineh, still terrorizing the people of Raithskar?" I demanded. My voice was shaking. I was very much afraid I would hear the very words she spoke next.

"You and Keeshah could return the stone to Raithskar," she said. "Without the cubs, you could make the trip quickly, deliver the Ra'ira to the Council, and—and return to Eddarta. Rikardon," she asked, pleading, "you *would* return to me in Eddarta?"

Tarani was as elegant and poised a woman as I had ever met, but she was young in biological age. All the anger I felt—which was, I was sure, an expression of fear of that proposed separation—faded before the protectiveness she inspired in those infrequent moments when she looked young and vulnerable, and let me see that she needed me.

She told the truth about not thinking this through before, I thought. *She's just had a glimpse of what it may really be like to become High Lord, and the responsibility is scaring her out of her wits.*

I sat beside her and put my arm around her shoulders. She turned her face against my chest and held me, trembling. We sat like that for a long time, and my thoughts rambled anxiously along lines toward the future.

Don't worry about it until it happens, I told myself.

As usual, I found it hard to listen to my own good advice.

We took leave of Lussim and his family early the next morning. Keeshah carried a freshly killed glith across his shoulders. Yaysha had a similar burden, and, as we climbed toward the Zantil Pass, my attention was thoroughly occupied with reminding the cubs that the food was for later.

Yoshah and Koshah were showing more endurance than I had hoped for. Apparently those first few weeks of growth had been a natural spurt, enough to get them large and coordinated enough to hunt for themselves. From here on out, it looked as if they would acquire their full size more gradually. We had allowed them to fast for the two days it had taken us to get from Thagorn to Relenor, and they seemed little harmed by it. They had eaten two heavy meals, and would have another before we tackled the Zantil Pass.

The Korchi mountain range separated the two large sections of Eddarta. They formed a rough triangle with its northernmost point merged into the Great Wall and its east-west base line formed by the Chizan crossing. There were two high passes, the Zantil on the west and the Zantro on the east, with an arid, hollow area nearly at the midpoint of the triangle's base. That hollow held Chizan, a city run exclusively by an element called the "rogueworld" in other cities. Travelers paid highly for anything they wanted, from water to gaming tokens, to hired assassination. A roguelord named Molik had controlled the city until Thymas killed him. The head man now was Worfit, a roguelord who had started out in Raithskar. Markasset had known him. I knew him. We were *not* friends. It had been Worfit and his men who had chased Tarani and me into the Well of Darkness, but Keeshah's appearance had daunted them.

After the sha'um had fed well, we started across the Zantil. It was an up, down, and up again trip, all in air so thin as to make breathing difficult and through winds that scoured and blinded with dust. When we reached the first crest, Tarani paused and pressed her arm to her chest, and I knew she was thinking of Lonna. The big white bird had been with her for years, and had made this crossing frequently, tucked inside Tarani's shirt.

I said nothing, knowing that I could only make her feel worse, and we started into the narrow, high-altitude valley. Tarani and I walked, each between an adult and a young sha'um. I kept a close watch on the cubs and tried to stay alert for any sign of fatigue.

As it turned out—and as I might have predicted, had I thought about it—the cubs came through in better shape than any of us. They had the more efficient lungs of sha'um, without the tremendous mass of their parents. They were irritated by the sand and bored with the slow pace, but they stuck with us. The six of us stumbled down the far side of the second crest a day and a half after we had topped the first one. We had moved slowly and steadily all that time, and all Tarani or I wanted was to lie down and sleep for a week or two. Keeshah and Yayshah were weary, but the clear air revived them. The cubs revived even quicker, and were soon complaining of hunger.

Rather than collapsing as we wanted to do, Tarani and I mounted the sha'um and nodded off during the trip to the outskirts of Chizan. We kept off the main road as much as possible, in order to avoid anyone seeing the sha'um. Worfit connected sha'um to me, and Worfit, I was sure, still wanted me.

We camped in a rocky depression, and I assured the cubs that food would arrive soon. Then I wrapped my face in the desert fashion—it was common practice in Chizan, and no one would think it odd. The hardest part came when I removed my baldric and handed Rika to Tarani.

"Will you go unarmed?" she asked.

I took back my dagger, and stuck it through my tunic's belt. "Have you forgotten the reward Worfit's offering for the man who carried the sword of *rakor*?" I asked. "Believe me, I'll be safer without it. I should be back soon."

I had tied all the water pouches together by their lacings. I shouldered the string of pouches and went into Chizan. Deliberately, I chose unfancy places to buy the water we needed—and was mildly surprised that the price had come down somewhat. Then I visited a vlek yard and bought three of the largest animals from an unsavory character who probably did not own them.

The sha'um prefer glith, I thought. *But they'll have to take what's available.*

I made it out of Chizan safely, and felt a slight letdown as

I led the vleks away from the city toward our camp. I felt angry too.

Worfit doesn't have to kill me, I thought. *He has already won by intimidation. Fear of him made me sneak in and out of Chizan, didn't it? That puts him in control.*

We were approaching the camp. The vleks caught the scent of the sha'um and went into their usual stamping, bawling frenzy. I couldn't hope to control them; I let them go, and called the sha'um to the hunt.

I watched Yoshah bring down one of the animals and thought, *One day, Worfit, you and I will have to settle what's between us.*

13

The Refreshment House at Iribos was our final stop before Eddarta. It was a bittersweet stay, because some of the Iribos Fa'aldu had been intimately involved in the ill-fated slave escape route. We took aside Veron, the young man we knew to be one of the activists, and told him the truth about the "safe house" in Chizan—that it was one and the same end destination of the less altruistic escape route that recruited dying slaves for the Living Death, a specialized, untraceable corps of assassins. The people helped by the Fa'aldu were recruited into the less savory areas of Chizan's rogueworld, or they were killed.

The Fa'aldu at Iribos already knew why we were there, of course. Not even sha'um could outrun the fast-flying maufa, dove-sized birds that carried messages in cleverly contrived breast pouches. The Fa'aldu were slightly amazed that we made no effort to conceal the sha'um from the travelers who came and went during the three days we stayed at Iribos, resting ourselves and the sha'um.

From the foot of the Zantro Pass (the second half of the Chizan Crossing), we had traveled in the same kind of rocky desert that lay between Relenor and Thagorn. We followed the southern wall of Gandalara which, unlike the Great Wall, was named in sections. To the far west, back beyond the Korchis, lay a section I had never seen but which had been identified on maps as the Wall of Mist. In the eastern half of Gandalara, there were the Rising Wall, which was a stairstep series of unattractive hills, climbing to impassable heights, the Desert Wall, which was more sheer and utterly dry, and the River Wall, which formed a miles-wide delta of fertile land and supported the largest city in Gandalara: Eddarta.

We might have made an easier trip if we had turned northward and followed the fertile crescent hugging the Korchis and the Great Wall. For part of that trip, there would be plentiful game for all the sha'um. But that route would have taken much longer, and carried the danger of running into one of the wild vineh colonies that sheltered in that same crescent.

So we had pushed the sha'um into fast crossings and long rests, and thoroughly abused the hospitality of the Fa'aldu. From Inid to Haddat to Kanlyr and now to Iribos—we had depended on the Fa'aldu for shelter and food, and they had given generously. We could not offer to pay, both because of the implied insult and because their tradition forbade the acceptance of coin. But Tarani and I were agreed that we would buy—not use her future position to acquire, but *buy*—something lovely and useful for each Refreshment House, and send them as gifts.

Tarani walked with me in the outer courtyard of the compound surrounded by walls built of salt blocks. It was the night before we were to leave for Eddarta. Light flickered from the oil lamps lining the wall, and we walked in and out of shadow.

"Indomel knows that we traveled with a Rider," she said, "and by now he knows that two Riders are approaching Eddarta. Do you think he knows who we are, or suspects these Riders are connected to us?"

I considered the question seriously. We had done very little planning for tomorrow's event, other than to ride boldly into Lord City and let Tarani state her claim to status among the Lords.

"Only Zefra knows that I'm Sharith," I said, "and Indomel is slow to give anyone else credit for a cunning that equals his. He might suspect that the rumors he's hearing mark a vengeance mission from our friends, but I think the fact that there are only two adult sha'um will ease that anxiety."

I smiled into the darkness.

"As a matter of fact, I'd give a lot to know what Indomel *is*— thinking about those rumors right now."

"Has it occurred to you," Tarani said, pausing by a salt-block ledge that, with the wall as backing, served as a bench, "that Indomel might know everything *we* are thinking?"

"It never crossed my mind," I said, truthfully. "Maybe that's only wishful thinking, but it seems to me that the kid had plenty of time to figure out how the Ra'ira works. If he couldn't use it when we left, he can't use it now."

She was quiet for a long time.

"Rikardon," she said at last, "I have thought about this a great deal. I feel sure that when I read the inscription on the Bronze, the Ra'ira had no part in it."

"What?" I said. "How can you be sure?"

She shrugged, obviously uncomfortable.

"It is difficult to explain—a feeling, an—an intuition, more than anything else. Mindpower is common in Gandalara in many forms, and some forms seem not far removed from the actual reading of thoughts. Why should it be possible, for instance, for me to *control* thought and cast illusion, but not to see the thoughts that are replaced by my projections? Does a maufel not guide his birds by imprinting a thought in their minds—the image of a place, or a person? The sha'um bond is thought *projection* primarily, but the bond is continuous and provides a constant exchange of feelings and attitudes.

"Yet the very specific skill of learning what another person *thinks* is not and never has been naturally present among us. Only the Ra'ira can activate that skill."

She lifted her hands, and clasped them together in front of her.

"I cannot believe that one could use the power of the Ra'ira unaware, without feeling close to it, bonded to it as you and Keeshah, Yayshah and I, are bonded. And I felt nothing of the sort when I read the Bronze. The stone in my hand felt inert and lifeless. If Indomel has not found the trigger for the stone's power, well, neither have I."

She sighed and dropped her arms.

"I believe the thought gladdens me."

* * *

We had left Raithskar surrounded by a crowd; we rode into Eddarta the same way.

We followed the main road, holding Yayshah and Keeshah to a walk and keeping the cubs between the adults. People stepped out of our way, stared at us curiously, swore at us as they fought to keep their vleks from going wild. Nobody asked us who we were. They knew, in an unreliable sort of way.

Some people in Eddarta had followed the raft that Thymas, Tarani, and I had "ridden" through the city, and had watched us meet two sha'um. Some other people had witnessed the procession of guards and dog-like dralda that had escorted Tarani and me back to Lord City. Some people were watching us arrive now, returning unescorted in the company of sha'um.

The odds were very good that *some* people had been in two or more of these groups, and were putting all the pieces together. I wasn't surprised to learn, from some strategic eavesdropping, that nobody knew exactly who we were, but folks were pretty sure we were the people who had killed the former High Lord.

Whether out of deference to the sha'um or out of agreement with that supposed action, no one tried to bar our entry into Eddarta. We followed the same route by which Obilin had brought us back in to Eddarta. A main city street ended at the foot of the broad single avenue that sloped up to Lord City, a walled area that housed the seven families who comprised the Lords of Eddarta. By the time I asked Keeshah to start uphill, we had a sizable following of curious people.

They kept a fair distance behind us and maintained a steady hum of conversation until we stopped in front of the entry gate. The guards—normally only one was on duty, but someone, on seeing this procession, had called out a squad of eight—watched us nervously as the biggest one stepped forward.

Tarani did not give him a chance to speak.

"Inform Indomel and the Lords," she said, in her clear, throaty voice, "that his elder sister has returned to Eddarta. Tell him to convene the Council at once, so that Tarani may be tested and proclaimed High Lord of Eddarta."

In the meaningless vernacular of Ricardo's world—it knocked their socks off.

The crowd roared and went running to spread the news. The guards stood as if turned to stone. One of them, recovering more quickly than the others, actually had the nerve to draw his sword.

By the time he had it out, Koshah was in front of him, snarling. The cub was a little less effective than Keeshah would have been, but the man backed up until he hit the stone wall, and then he dropped his sword and flattened his empty hands against the wall. He looked familiar.

"You," I called to him. "What is your name?"

His mouth worked silently for a minute, and finally he croaked: "N-Nulan."

"Do you remember me, Nulan?" I asked, edging Keeshah closer and calling Koshah to step back a little. The other guards made room for us.

"Y-yes," the man said. "Sir."

"You knew me as Lakad," I reminded him. "And you kept me locked up, on Obilin's orders, for nearly a seven-day."

"O-Obilin ain't here no more. Sir."

"I know."

I said it softly, but I was sure every guard in that squad heard not only the words, but the truth behind them—that I had good reason to know why Obilin was no longer there.

I whirled Keeshah to face the man who had stepped out front. He would be in charge of the squad.

"What are your orders concerning us?" I asked him.

He looked at me, at Tarani, and at each of the sha'um. He started to smile, and then his face went rigid, his sword came out, and he launched himself—not at me or Keeshah, but at Tarani, who was seated with Yayshah's flank facing the guard.

Yoshah intercepted him, her jaws closing around the extended sword arm. The man gave a yell and tumbled aside, rolling over and under the sha'um.

Yoshah, that's enough! I called, fighting for control of the young mind that had slipped into battle madness. *Come away, Yoshah, come back, girl!*

She backed away from the prostrate and now unconscious man, whose mangled arm still kept a mockery of a

97

grip on the sword that had been aimed, unmistakably, for Tarani's heart.

Tarani looked down at the body, and her anger flared.

"Look at him," she ordered the other guards, "and see your High Lord. For it was he who ordered the attack. It was Indomel who *compelled* this man to risk his life." She stared around at the guards, forcing each one to meet her gaze. "Indomel fears me," she said, "but not because he knows my claim is true. He fears me because I have my own strength, and have no need of the unwilling service of others.

"This man was compelled," she repeated. "Are there any among you who wish, of your own will, to destroy me?"

Surprisingly, Nulan stepped away from the wall and spoke. "Er, ma'am, I just thought you'd like to know—the High Lord told us to keep you out of Lord City. Just that, and nothin' more. We was offered a bonus if we did it, and—and death if we failed."

Tarani swung her left leg over Yayshah's back and slid to the ground, landing with lithe grace. She walked over to face the man. I—and the three sha'um who knew what I felt—got *very* tense.

"Nulan, is it?" Tarani asked him. Nulan swallowed and nodded. "I thank you for speaking honestly, Nulan. I know the law of the Lords. When the identity of the High Lord is in question, no one fills that position. That means that once I have entered Lord City, Indomel has no authority until he is re-acclaimed by the Council at the midday meeting—if that happens.

"He will not be re-acclaimed," she said. "Do you believe me?"

Nulan nodded again. Around him, I saw other guards nod their heads, and wondered briefly whether Tarani was using her own kind of compulsion. I rejected that idea; what I was seeing was an ordinary group of men totally fascinated by an extraordinary woman. She had a personal power that, at times, was even stronger than her mindpower.

"Even if Indomel tries to violate the law, I and my friends can protect you from him. Do you believe me?" she asked again.

More nods.

"Then I ask you, in the name of your own law, to admit Tarani, daughter of Zefra and Pylomel, to the city of her family."

Nulan started to speak, then his eyes went glassy and his hands leaped for her throat.

Damn! I thought.

Tarani's body blocked all the sha'um from her attacker, and she wasn't moving.

After a split second, neither was Nulan.

He stopped with his hands on her throat, but not closing. He looked like a man for whom time had suddenly stopped. His face was tormented, and his arms trembled, and suddenly I understood.

She's counteracting Indomel's compulsion! Telling Nulan, with equal force, not to do what Indomel is ordering.

14

Even as I finally figured it out, Nulan's eyes cleared. He lowered his hands, and he stepped back from Tarani, looking embarrassed. Tarani, tension clear in every muscle of her body, turned toward the open gate.

"Indomel," she called. "You have failed. If you have a shred of dignity left, then come to the gate, and relieve these men of their orders."

We all waited, holding our breath—me, Tarani, the seven remaining guards, four sha'um, and nearly two hundred awestruck Eddartans.

"If you make no claim on dignity, then I shall offer you none," Tarani said at last.

A whimpering sound came from the gateway. From behind the wall on the left, moving stiffly, appeared a tall, slim young man who bore a noticeable resemblance to Tarani—except for the look of fanatic hatred and dawning fear in his eyes.

Tarani's eyes were glowing.

One of the prerequisites for being High Lord was possession of a strong degree of mindpower, and it was clear to everyone there that Tarani had imposed *her* power on the present High Lord. She brought him into the center of the gateway and asked again: "Do you believe I can protect you from Indomel's reprisals, if you admit me to Lord City?"

Lots of nods.

"But they hold no true right of admittance or restriction," came a voice from inside the walls.

The gateway opened onto a cobbled walkway that led to the building called Lord Hall, which rested at the center of eight radiant walkways. The other seven led to areas belonging to each of the seven Lord families. I had been so preoccupied with what was happening outside the walls that I had not noticed a crowd gathering on the inside as well. It was a much smaller crowd, true. But six men who looked very official stepped out to stand beside Indomel. Each wore a white tunic embroidered with an emblem at the left shoulder. The two on either side of Indomel quietly took hold of his arms.

The deep and cultured voice came again, from the man directly on Indomel's right. He was middle-aged, tall, with slightly rounded shoulders.

"Release Indomel," the man said, without letting it sound like a command.

The glow faded from Tarani's eyes, and Indomel sagged as if he had been hovering four inches off the ground. He sagged, recovered, snarled like an animal, and would have jumped at Tarani—and discovered he was being held. He looked around in surprise, and made a poor effort to cover what had just happened.

"Why, Hollin," he said to the man who had spoken, "I was just . . ." His voice broke off as he saw the two men beside Hollin, then whipped his head around to look at the other three. "But it was not necessary for all of you to come out here," he stammered in a trembling voice, and he uttered a chittering, obviously false, laugh. "You with your bad knee, Mosor, you walked so far?"

"Enough, Indomel," Hollin said. He seemed to be the senior member of the group. "It is clear enough what happened here. This lady claims kinship to you, and has demonstrated an impressive mindgift. She acted within the law in requesting the assembly of the Council, and a fair test. You—" The cultured voice broke, and resumed with its note of contempt not quite under control. "You have shown yourself to be a spiteful coward."

He turned Indomel's arm over to the next man, who gripped it with both hands. Hollin stepped forward, outside the gate, and extended his palm, turned up, toward Tarani.

"I, Hollin of Shegan, invite you to Lord Hall to present your claim before the Council. Your name, if you please."

"I am Tarani of Harthim," she said, and then surprised him by adding: "and of the Sharith. Will the Council admit my companion, the Captain of the Sharith, to the Council proceedings?"

I tried to keep my face expressionless.

After a long pause, Hollin spoke up.

"It is hardly usual, but the situation carries a substantial weight of oddness," he said. "If you both understand that he may observe only, I think his attendance can be permitted."

"No!" Indomel shouted, and started jerking his body violently between the two men who held him, trying to free himself. "Do not be deceived by that slut," he shouted, shocking everyone. "She is the daughter of a *jeweler* and not my true sister!"

He continued ranting for a few seconds, while the crowd behind him parted to let a woman, of medium height with a very pronounced widow's peak of dark fur, to come to the front of the group.

"Members of the Council, you know me. I am Zefra, mother to Indomel and widow to Pylomel. I tell you now that I am also mother to Tarani, and that she *is* the daughter of Pylomel." Indomel started to scream curses at her, but Zefra maintained her poise—though I noticed she blinked her eyes a little too rapidly, and the flesh of her neck quivered.

"I say again, Tarani is Indomel's true sister, and first-born of Pylomel. I ask only that the Council test her. The choice of High Lord is the Council's alone."

Hollin was still standing with his hand out to Tarani. She accepted it, and held her other hand out to me. I slid down from Keeshah's back, and greeted Hollin with a brief bow. We stepped through the gate, and Zefra greeted her daughter with a shining look and a kiss on the cheek.

Me, she nodded to.

Indomel, who had settled down to a morose sulk, was transferred to the care of Nulan and another guard, and everyone inside the city walls turned around and headed for Lord Hall.

I had the feeling that the crowd outside the walls was growing, rather than dispersing, and they would settle in and wait for the decision to be announced.

Keeshah and the two cubs, at my direction, headed for the wild country on the slopes above Lord City. Yayshah went along, either just to stay with the family or because Tarani had sent her.

Lord Hall was a vast, octagonal building, hollow except for the rectangular Council chamber that stood at its center. The outer shell had eight doors; the Council chamber had only one. Hollin guided the group of Lords and others (including me) through the milling crowd to the narrow corridor that led to the only visible entry to the Council chamber.

Hollin raised his hands, and the crowd fell silent. "Only the Lords, the candidates, and the witnesses may enter the Council Chamber," he announced. "Our decision will be imparted to you as soon as it is reached."

Hollin looked sternly at Indomel.

"Will you disgrace the Council by requiring the presence of guards, or will you give your oath to behave with the dignity of a Lord?"

Indomel glared at him. "You have my oath, Hollin."

Hollin nodded to the guards, who let go of Indomel's arms. Hollin led the way through the normal door that opened into one end of a rectangular room, turning to nod agreement to the guards entering with Indomel. A table and six high-backed chairs stood on the floor. At the near end of the table was a featureless stool. At the far end of the room was a raised platform, a seventh chair that stood higher by the height of the platform, and an enormous sheet of bronze that covered a six-foot span from ceiling to floor.

I wonder if the Lords know that the Bronze conceals the door to the treasure vault, which surrounds this room on three sides? I thought. *Probably not. Probably that's a secret passed from one High Lord to another—unnecessary, in this case, since Tarani already knows about it.*

Zefra and I stood in one rear corner of the room; Indomel in the other corner, with the distance of the entry door between us. Tarani stood at the foot of the table, very

103

deliberately *not* sitting on the stool meant for the fifteen-year-olds who were possible candidates for High Lord.

The other Lords took their places along both sides of the table, with Hollin on the right, nearest to the Bronze. He stood up, held his hand out toward the Bronze, and said: "This is the test, Tarani. Please read what you can of the markings on the Bronze."

The huge sheet of bronze, mounted on part of the wall, was imprinted with rows and rows of an identical eight-part character, some combination of which made up the alphabet characters of the Gandalaran language. Zanek, the First King, had asked a craftsman to stamp a message on the bronze, and then go back and fill in the missing parts of each character, to make all the figures look exactly alike.

The theory seemed to be that, if you had a strong mindgift, you also had a strong subconscious link with the All-Mind, and could reach back to the moment of engraving to distinguish the first layer of lettering from the added marks. Zanek had made the reading of the Bronze—at least part of it—a portion of the ceremony by which he transferred the power of the Kingdom into the hands of a new King. That tradition, like many others, had been garbled in Eddarta into making reading of the Bronze a test for mindpower.

In point of fact, the Bronze was so old by now that the ability to read more than three words was counted as evidence of a strong mindpower. Therefore, when Tarani read out loud in a clear, if slightly shaky, voice . . .

> *I greet thee in the name of the new Kingdom.*
> *From chaos have we created order.*
> *From strife have we enabled peace.*
> *From greed have we encouraged sharing.*

. . . well, it knocked their socks off.

She hesitated briefly, and I knew she was skipping the part about the Sharith and the Ra'ira. She covered it well, and resumed the reading:

> **THIS IS THE TASK I GIVE THEE**
> **AS FIRST DUTY**

As you read the scholar's meaning
Within the craftsman's skill,
So read within yourself
Your commitment

> *To guide*
> *To lead*
> *To learn*
> *To protect.*

If you lack a high need
To improve life for all men,
Then turn aside now,
For you would fail the Kingdom.

I greet thee in the name of the new Kingdom,
And I charge thee: care for it well.

> *I am Zanek,*
> *King of Gandalara.*

When she had finished reading, there was absolute silence in the room.

I glanced at Indomel, who was staring at his sister with something like awe. *He really thought the Ra'ira helped her to read that inscription,* I realized. *I think it is finally dawning on him how powerful she really is.*

But Indomel had not given up.

"The mindgift of this woman is conceded," he said. "And I give no opposition to accepting her as the daughter of Zefra. Yet you are all aware that Zefra's regard for me bears little resemblance to the caring of a mother. I believe that, in claiming Tarani to be the daughter of my father, she seeks only to see me removed from my position."

Zefra sputtered, and I put a hand on her arm. She jerked her arm away, but kept silent.

"We have heard Zefra's testimony," Hollin said, and looked around at the other Lords, "but Indomel's doubt is, I believe, fair." Indomel was nearly himself again, and he showed no reaction to that gesture of approval. "The candidate's parentage seems to be an unattainable truth, yet she is clearly qualified and continues to have the right of consideration through her connection to Zefra."

Hollin sat down, and another Lord stood up. This one was older, not quite as tall as Hollin, and just a trifle paunchy. He, too, had a rich-sounding voice, but there was something less palatable about him.

Perhaps it was the way he glanced at Indomel an instant before he began speaking. I read it as an "Okay, here's the one I owe you" kind of a look.

"It appears to me that what we have here is an equal contest," he said. "The lady Tarani has demonstrated a superior mindpower, yet Indomel has the only uncontested claim to a legitimate heritage. With such a balance, it is our decision, my friends, and I say that we must keep the welfare of Eddarta clearly in view as we consider our choice.

"Indomel has lived among us all his life, and has proven to be a capable and effective administrator. Have not the profits from the copper mines increased greatly since his installation as High Lord? Do we not get quick and fair decisions on any matter we take to him?

"I will not say that Indomel has no weaknesses," the eloquent Lord went on, gesturing toward Indomel with an air of having touched him companionably on the shoulder. "Yet High Lords are first Lords, and Lords are first and only people. Who among us would not admit to weakness in some area?

"I say that Indomel is familiar, and experienced, and the one called Tarani," he said, bowing toward the girl, "is a stranger to us, with an imperfect claim. Are we willing to turn over our loyalty—and our resources—to a stranger who has great strength, but who is untrained in our ways and unfamiliar with our needs?"

It was an effective speech, calling up the fears of the greedy Lords. I knew of at least one case in which a candidate had been refused because he had *too* powerful a mindgift.

If I had been capable of it physically, I would have started sweating. Tarani, however, seemed totally in control.

"May I speak, Lords?" Tarani asked.

Indomel's friend had been in the act of sitting down. Hollin rose smoothly to field Tarani's question.

"The other candidate has spoken freely, Tarani. You may say whatever you wish."

"Sarel has offered sound advice," she said, startling everyone by using the man's name.

She must have learned a lot about Lords and Eddartan law from Zefra while I was "involved" at the Lingis mine, I thought.

"It is true," Tarani continued, "that my knowledge of present-day Eddarta is limited. Yet I know a great deal about the source from which it sprang." She drew her sword, causing a twitch or two around the table, and held it at arm's length, horizontally, so that there could be no doubt of the sword's material. It was made of rakor—the Gandalaran word for the iron and tin alloy Ricardo would have called steel—and it gleamed with a silver light that drew all eyes to it.

"This sword is the King's sword," she said, "lost since Harthim abandoned Kä and came here. I have walked in the streets of Kä, and shared the lifememory of some who lived there. And I learned well the lesson Sarel teaches." Her voice became softer, very gentle. "I believed Harthim to be evil, but I touched his memory and found that he was merely the creation of his time. I believed Zanek to be good, and strong, and found in him the weakness of a normal man. I knew that only two qualities are indispensable in a leader: a willingness to work harder than everyone else; and the ability to learn from, correct, and then forget mistakes. And I began to think that I might have those qualities.

"I shall not lie before the Council of Lords," she said. "As a child, I was taught by a man who had bitter memories of Eddarta and a lingering hatred of the Lords. I believed as he did, because I—because I loved and trusted him, and I thought he was my father. When I learned that Pylomel had sired me I was first appalled, and then resolved to reach for the position of High Lord as a means to revenge."

Tarani put away the sword, and opened her empty hands toward the Lords.

"I have no such motive now, my Lords. I shall not say that I have lost the prejudices taught me by Volitar, or that I wholly approve of all I have seen in Eddarta. Yet I *will* say that I believe Eddarta, Lords and landservants both, will profit from your acceptance of me as High Lord.

"I have come here because I accept Eddarta as part of my heritage, and I want to free the city of the devious and selfish leadership of Indomel."

Indomel started, and his eyes narrowed. Hollim noticed, and flashed him a warning look. The boy's lips pressed into a thin line as Tarani continued.

"Sarel rightly cites my ignorance of Eddartan ways. Then who shall teach me? Who but the Council of Lords? Think what it will be like to have a High Lord who listens to each of you equally, and makes a judgment impartially, free of generations of favor trades and 'special arrangements.'

"Sarel cleverly implied that the Lords might do well to fear my mindgift. I tell you now that you need fear me much less than Indomel, for danger lies in use. I was taught, and I continue to believe, that using mindpower to lead another person into harm is a deed of incomparable evil that degrades both user and used. You witnessed the events of a few minutes ago. Who, in that exchange, used mindpower for aggression, and who only in defense? The Council has my word that I shall never imitate my brother. I shall not use my mindgift to humiliate or harm another person, or to gain agreement from an unwilling Lord."

The men around the table looked uneasily at one another. Indomel saw the exchange, and a muscle in his cheek started to twitch.

"I make one last point, my Lords. Sarel has said that the balance between my proven mindgift and Indomel's proven birthright is even, and he offers you the security of the known in Indomel's favor. I offer two things to be considered in the balance.

"First, I bring you the *unknown*, and with it the *opportunity* for change, with my promise I shall learn what is before I offer alternatives.

"Second, the sword of the Kings has returned to light in my hand. I believe that to be both confirmation of my right to lead and an omen of renewed prosperity for the descendants of the Kings.

"Indomel and Tarani bid to be High Lord," she finished. "The Lords must choose who they will follow."

15

"Lies!" Indomel exploded. "She speaks only the vicious lies she heard from Zefra, that dralda who claims to be *her* mother and . . . *my* . . . mother. . . ."

Indomel's voice trailed off, as he realized what he was saying.

Beside me, Zefra smiled.

Hollin leaned over the table and looked down it toward Indomel and Tarani. "You are a stranger to me, Tarani," he said.

I thought back, and realized that while a large population in Lower Eddarta had seen us coming into the city, only Indomel's guards had seen us *inside* Lord City. *If you don't count our breakneck escape from Eddarta the night Thymas killed Pylomel, that is,* I thought. *Everybody in Lord Hall that night was too busy panicking to get a good look at us.*

Hollin's statement seemed to require some sort of answer. Tarani nodded.

"Where did you gain your knowledge of Eddartan law, and how did you learn of what you claim to be your true parentage?"

"I learned the identity of my mother," she said, "from a single letter sent to Volitar from Eddarta, hoarded as a man cherishes a great treasure. It is from Zefra that I have learned all else that pertains to Eddarta."

"Zefra," Hollin said. Tarani's mother stepped away from me to stand beside her daughter.

"Yes, Hollin."

110

"Am I mistaken in my belief that, until today, you have not left the home of the High Lord without escort since your return to Eddarta, twenty years ago?"

"You are not mistaken, Hollin," Zefra answered, tossing her head back. "I have been imprisoned, first by my husband, and then by my son. I thank you for your assistance in freeing me today."

Zefra said she had "contacts," I thought. Hollin must be one of them. But Zefra, obviously, has not told him about Tarani. Good move, I'd guess. Hollin seems a fair man. If he thought Zefra had tried to pre-influence him for this decision, he would have less respect for Tarani.

"Will you explain," Hollin said, "how you were able to share your knowledge with your daughter?"

"Tarani joined my imprisonment, Hollin. We were together for nearly a moon, and learned much of each other in that time."

"Who was High Lord during that period?" Hollin asked, with an increased tension in his voice.

"Indomel," Zefra said. "I dare to anticipate your next question, Hollin. Indomel had been told the same truth I spoke outside—that Tarani is Pylomel's firstborn child."

Hollin fairly roared at Indomel: "Confirm or deny!"

The boy jumped in fright, shrank back, then straightened his shoulders and regained a shred of composure.

"Confirmed," he said. "What my *mother* leaves out is that Tarani came to Lord City as a thief, intending to steal the—uh, the High Lord's treasure. I apprehended her and, out of consideration of her possible family connection to me, chose to detain her in the comfort of Zefra's apartments, rather than assign her to one of the mines."

Indomel stepped toward the center of his end of the table, crowding Zefra.

"Be aware, fellow Lords, that theft remains her goal even now, as she presses this preposterous claim."

A pair of hands slapped the tile-topped table, and we all jumped at the sound. The Lord seated nearest Tarani, an old man with only a wispy fringe remaining around a nearly bald pate, scraped back his chair and stood up.

"Forgive me, Lord Hollin," he said in a scratchy, no-nonsense voice, "but I am too old to stand on ceremony

111

when it is not necessary. What we have here is an insoluble matter of *opinion*, with no way to tell who is and who is not lying. The lady Zefra," he said, with a bobbing bow in her direction, "while she is loved by us all, is known to have been—ah—erratic in the past and—ah—somewhat in conflict with the High Lord. I hasten to say that I personally believe Zefra, but I hesitate to base a Council decision solely on her statements."

He cleared his throat.

"Great Harthim," he muttered, as if to himself, "I am getting to be as bad as everyone else."

He continued more loudly. "To—ah—get to the point quickly, only three things I have heard today were worth listening to. One was the reading of the Bronze." The old man bowed to Tarani. "For that I thank you, my dear. The second was Sarel's evaluation that, by ordinary means of judging, Indomel and Tarani are equally qualified to be High Lord. And the third, my friends, the third was Tarani's assessment of the qualities of leadership.

"The lady has been called a thief. Would anyone here deny that Indomel has been called worse things?"

A few snickers, quickly muffled, sounded around the table.

"Lord Hollin, you are the expert on the rules, but it seems to me that this situation calls for a vote. I shall claim the privilege of age and give you mine now, to spare these old bones the chore of standing up again.

"I recommend the Council choose Tarani."

The old man sat down.

One by one, the other Lords stood up and voted for Tarani. It was unanimous. Indomel watched each Lord with wild eyes, and when the sixth vote was cast, he started to shout.

"You fools!" he yelled. "She will dominate you all. She knows how to use the—the—the—"

His eyes bulged and he stopped trying to talk. His hands flew to his throat and he made ineffectual gasping motions with his mouth.

Tarani scrambled around her mother to support the boy as he struggled for air, then looked sternly at Zefra and said, "Stop it."

Zefra's face shone with triumph and vindication, and in her eyes burned the glow of mindpower.

"Stop it, Mother!" Tarani ordered again.

She was taller and looked stronger than the sallow boy who had been High Lord of Eddarta—who was on the verge of passing out. The Lord beside them had stood up in alarm, and Tarani passed the ailing boy into his hands. Zefra's eyes followed Indomel's movement.

Tarani took one step toward her mother and delivered a perfect right cross. Zefra flew back into the old Lord's lap, and Indomel started breathing—noisily. Tarani glanced at me, and I remembered how to move. Together we pulled Zefra off the flustered old man, each of us draping one of her arms over our shoulders.

"As Zefra said, she and I had time to get to know one another during the period of my imprisonment," Tarani said, addressing the Lords. "Her life of solitude has left her unbalanced on the side of hatred and vengeance. I will not allow her to express those feelings through abuse of her power."

She glanced at Indomel, who had all he could do to stay on his feet.

"I accept the place you offer me with gratitude and great hope for the future, my Lords. Hollin, I will appreciate your seeing to whatever has to be done officially. I shall take Zefra to the Harthim residence and begin the process of making it my home. When Indomel is sufficiently recovered, please ask the guards to escort him there, as well.

"Rikardon," she said (and it was my ego, and not her voice, that made it seem an afterthought), "will reside with us. On the third day from now, let us meet here again, and begin my education. For now, gentlemen, good day."

Hollin came out of the Council chamber ahead of us and held back an intensely curious crowd while Tarani and I dragged her mother out of Lord Hall and down the walkway leading to the Harthim family area, and the huge and rambling structure in which the High Lord traditionally lived. Hollin must have given some kind of signal, because a squad of the High Guard—until recently at the command of Indomel—followed us at a respectful distance.

113

"Zefra is going to be furious when she wakes up," I whispered.

"And she will meet a greater fury," Tarani said grimly. "How bitter that the first act to take place under my leadership should be attempted murder, through compulsion. I dared not even *speak* to her, Rikardon," she said, "much less begin to counteract the compulsion, as I did at the city gates. My anger was too great."

"You handled it in the best way possible," I assured her. And then, because I did not like Zefra very much and felt a trifle guilty about that, I said: "I suspect her anger got away from her, too, and that all she started out to do was keep Indomel from mentioning—"

I prudently left the word unsaid, and Tarani looked at me over her mother's head and smiled, just a little. "Thank you for saying that, Rikardon. I will make an effort to see the incident as kindly as you do." Her gaze rested for a moment on her mother's head, which wobbled slightly with the concussion of our steps. "It would be ironic, would it not, if I felt forced to continue Zefra's imprisonment?"

We had reached the entry to the Harthim area, which was an opening between two barracks buildings. The two men on guard stepped toward the center of the path to block our way, then caught sight of the honor guard behind us and separated again. They offered to help with Zefra, but we declined. She was a small burden for the two of us, and I suspected that Tarani relished the contact with her mother.

The back entrance to the big house lay just beyond the barracks. We went inside and wound through the twisting, unpredictable corridors to Zefra's room. I left Tarani alone with Zefra, and wandered off on my own.

I was looking for, and wanted badly, a flask of barut.

That wasn't so bad, I thought. *If you're fond of tension and you enjoy confrontation.*

I snagged a servant who replied to my request for directions with a mumbled answer and a reluctance to look me in the face, then hurried off. Following his guidance, I found the sitting room close to the front of the house, in which Indomel had conducted a memorably uncomfortable interview, just before he sent me off to serve at the Lingis copper mine.

The refreshments I sought were there, and I helped myself.

There was also an ornamented wooden box—the same one in which I had seen Indomel place the Ra'ira on my last occasion in this room.

Nah, I thought. *It can't be that easy.*

I had my hand on the box when someone knocked at the door, scaring me into spilling barut on the woven carpet.

"Yes?" I called.

The door opened and a guard stepped in, holding a droopy-looking Indomel by one elbow.

"As the High Lord commanded," the guard said stiffly, "Indomel has been brought to the house of Harthim. Are there further instructions?"

You're asking me? I thought.

Indomel looked like a man with a broken spirit, but I had good reason to respect the boy's capacity for deceit.

"Take him to one of the—uh—spare rooms, and set a guard on his door. The High Lord will provide further instructions later."

The guard nodded and started back out the door, pulling Indomel with him. I felt relieved that he had accepted my authority to give that kind of direction, and a little chagrined at having been put in the place of Assistant High Lord.

Indomel resisted the guard's movement, dragging himself backward and holding on to the door sill. He looked me full in the face, and I thought: *He lost, and it hurts—but he's not down. I must remember to warn Tarani, if she doesn't already know not to trust the kid.*

Indomel's gaze flickered from me to the box and back again.

"Enjoy it," he whispered, "for all the good it may do you. It is barren and useless."

The guard dragged him away.

I opened the box, and took out a palm-sized blue stone: the Ra'ira.

16

It was dark by the time I saw Tarani again that day. I was still in the sitting room, and doing a good imitation of Dharak. Tarani opened the door and looked in, then came through the closed door. She touched me, leaned down to kiss me lightly, then settled onto a divan and sighed heavily. We were both still wearing the clothes in which we had arrived—desert tunic and trousers.

One lamp was burning in the room, the candle flame brightened by the facets in the glass chimney surrounding it. Tarani lay her head back and closed her eyes. After a moment or two, she roused again.

"Did you eat something?" she asked me.

"Yes, one of the—uh—"

"*Servants*," she said, emphasizing the word. "I have made it clear to the head of household maintenance that no slaves will be permitted in this house." She shrugged. "A small beginning which will not threaten the other Lords, but speaks for the changes I desire to make."

"One day as High Lord," I said, "and you are already thinking like a statesman. Yes, one of the servants found me in here, took pity, and brought me some dinner. What about you? Have you had time to eat?"

She looked at me sharply.

"This room is near the front entry, remember. I've heard the traffic; I know you've been busy. I kept expecting to be moved out of here, so you could use this room for meetings, or whatever."

"Things never quite reached that degree of formality,"

116

Tarani said, rubbing a hand across her eyes. "I stayed with Zefra until she woke, and we had a moment of the fury you predicted. Then she became remorseful, and we were finally able merely to greet one another as mother and daughter.

"I saw Indomel briefly—thank you for the arrangements you made, by the way; they exactly matched my intent—and assured him he would remain here, in a degree of confinement that corresponds to his proven trustworthiness.

"Hollin called on me to discuss the public transfer of power—a Celebration Dance will be held in two-days' time.

"I have had a brief meeting with each of the other Lords. It is odd, Rikardon; I find them to be largely well-intentioned men who support the Eddartan system because it is what they know. They represent the interests of their families with care and honor. One or two—Sarel, in particular—seem to be more willing to be greedy for themselves than for their families. They are intelligent people, and open to new ideas. I see much that can be done here, Rikardon."

There was a fervor in her voice I had never heard before. I sipped my third small glass of barut, and let her talk until she wound down and noticed my silence.

She laughed self-consciously.

"Forgive me for prattling, my love. This has been an exciting day, a new beginning for me." She got up and went to pour her own glass of barut.

She saw the ornate box. She set down the flask and opened the box, and gasped a little as she took out the stone and held it toward the lamp. The candlelight shimmered along the stone's intricate structure lines, casting a refracted blue glow back over Tarani's face.

She closed her hand around the gem, and turned to me.

"This is the reason you have stayed in here all day, is it not? You were guarding the stone."

I shook my head.

"I was thinking," I corrected her. "About many things, some of them very personal. But I was thinking a lot about *that*." I nodded toward the hand that held the Ra'ira.

I stood up, took her arm, and guided her to stand by the window and look out into the huge garden. By the light of an oil lamp, a gardener was pouring water from a ceramic jug into an irrigation channel.

"Try to tell me what that man is thinking," I said.

She stared at me.

"Go on," I urged. "I'd offer myself as a test, but we've already seen that my mind is different, and less accessible."

"I—all right. I will try."

She certainly seemed to try. Her body went tense, her eyes closed, and lines of effort appeared in her forehead. After a moment, she relaxed and inhaled deeply.

"I feel nothing," she said.

"I've been putting things together," I said. "Indomel has a lot of power, yet he was never able to use the stone." She looked at me in surprise and I explained: "He told me so himself, when he arrived this afternoon. He would have no reason to lie about it.

"You said, in Iribos, that you believed the Ra'ira would have some *special* feeling to it when it was used—and you've just now proved that your greater power can't activate it."

Tarani pushed me away from the window and paced across the room. She opened her hand and stared at the blue jewel.

"It could be a trick of learning," she said. But her voice sounded doubtful, and I knew that her mind had admitted the same terrifying suspicion that had plagued me all afternoon.

"Tarani, I have *used* the Ra'ira," I said, startling her. "Not as myself, but while I shared the lifememory of Zanek. I was there at the moment he discovered the power. There was no trick, no combination of factors to be perfectly arranged. He held the stone, and could hear the thoughts of the people around him as clearly as he could hear their voices.

"Think back to the lifememory of Serkajon that you and I shared in Kä. When Zanek appeared in Serkajon's memory as a Visitor, he used the Ra'ira's power to watch the movement of the guards while he stole the gem from Harthim's bedroom. Do you recall that? How little effort it

118

took to make the thing work? As soon as he was near the stone, he could use it."

She was nodding. "Yes, I do remember," she said, frowning. "But Zanek's power was born of an earlier age," she protested. "Perhaps the modern mindgift is not strong enough—" She paused. She held up her hand to caution me against interrupting her thoughts. "Obviously, the Supervisors in Raithskar have been able to use the Ra'ira's power on the vineh. But I see a qualitative difference between seeing an animal's intent to violence and understanding the rational thought of a man. Perhaps the Kings had a different sort of power, and it has been lost in the years since the Kingdom fell."

"Here in Eddarta," I reminded her, "the Lords have been doing what amounts to keeping the breed lines pure, to encourage the presence of mindgifts among the Lord families. Logic would support the existence of a stronger, not a weaker, mindgift."

"Uh—and speaking of breed lines, isn't there a rule that says the High Lord has to marry a member of one of the Lord families?"

Tarani walked over to the refreshment area and poured the barut she had wanted earlier. "Is that the 'personal' thing you have been thinking about?" she asked.

"One of them," I hedged. "Is there a rule, or not?"

"You know very well that such a rule exists," she said. She turned around, leaned on the stone wall into which the refreshment shelf was cut, and sipped her drink. "It will be changed—if it becomes necessary."

"*If?*" I sputtered. "*If* it becomes necessary?"

"Rikardon, my love," she said, in a deadly calm voice. "Think carefully. Have you ever spoken to me of marriage?"

I gaped at her, my heart racing with confusion and apprehension.

"Have I ever led you to believe," I finally said, "that I wanted *anything* more than for us to continue to be together?"

"Once, and recently," she said. "At Relenor, we discussed the need for separation—you to take *this*"—she tossed the blue stone lightly—"back to Raithskar, I to fill the role I have chosen here in Eddarta."

119

"We discussed the *possibility*!" I whirled away from her and paced around the room, trying to calm myself. When I felt more in control, I faced Tarani again. "The possibilities are vastly changed," I said, "if this stone is *not* the true Ra'ira."

An odd thing happens when you talk out loud about something you fear. It becomes more real, more frightening, and yet it seems easier to deal with it, once it has been expressed.

Tarani straightened up and set her empty glass on the shelf. "If this is not the real stone, where is it?"

"Now *that* is mostly what I've been thinking about all day. I've gone over my memory of every second we were in contact with Gharlas, every time we have seen *any* version of the Ra'ira. Every way I look at it, I see the same thing: Gharlas *believed* he had the real thing. He would not have let it out of his sight. The jewel we took from his body was the same one he had brought all the way from Raithskar."

"Can we be sure that *this* is that same stone?" she asked.

"I'd bet on it," I said. "Gharlas said that Volitar made only two realistic copies of the Ra'ira."

"Are you saying," she demanded, "that this is the second copy? Gharlas also said that it was lost—"

"In Raithskar," I interrupted. "Where someone who had the *real* Ra'ira could easily send a vineh to pick it up and deliver it somewhere. He switched the duplicate for the real stone during his duty shift, then held his own private duty shift to convince the next custodian that the jewel in the vault was the real thing."

Tarani took a couple of steps away from me, came back, paced away again. "If we suppose that the situation you described is true, then the real thief is a Supervisor who used Gharlas to draw attention away from himself." She threw up her hands. "For what possible reason? I have no doubt that Gharlas was cleverly guided, but he obviously believed in everything he said to us. He was entirely mad, of course, but he did seem to have a reason for wanting the Ra'ira. The thief you propose would have *had* the gem in his possession a good part of the time. Why steal it?"

I shrugged. "I haven't a clue," I said. "The way I've

worked it out, it could have been any one of the Supervisors—though my preference is to rule out Thanasset as a possibility. One, I don't believe he *would* do such a thing. Two, the thing was stolen during his duty shift, and he's certainly smarter than that. I've listed the Supervisors a dozen times in my head, trying to figure out why. I know that two of them are having financial problems right now. Another just lost his wife in childbirth, and seemed to go a little crazy for a while. But there's nothing certain, nothing I can pin down."

"Let us leave it, then," Tarani suggested, "and address a different question. If this *is* one of Volitar's duplicates, and not the true Ra'ira, what then? What are the possibilities which you see as vastly changed?"

"I—uh—well—ah—"

She crossed her arms and waited, not giving me any help at all. I cleared my throat and started again. "Um—well, the way I see it, you'll need to come back to Raithskar with me."

"I see," she said.

"Do you?" I asked her. I moved closer, and took her upper arms in my hands. The muscles were taut and strong. "We made a commitment to make the Ra'ira safe from abuse again. How often have we talked about that being our 'destiny'?"

I drew my hand along her arm to her hand, and took the blue gemstone to hold it up between us.

"If this *is* real, then—yes, sending me back to Raithskar alone would satisfy the commitment, and you could get on with your life as the High Lord." I was surprised by a surge of bitterness—jealousy?—that showed in my voice so clearly that Tarani flinched away and strode across the room.

"If this is *not* real, then—we're not finished yet, Tarani, not until the Ra'ira has been taken back to the *Council* of Supervisors, first to protect Raithskar from the vineh, and then to be destroyed, or isolated, or handled in whatever way is necessary to keep it from ever being used again."

When Tarani spoke, her words seemed unrelated to the topic. "You were not born among the Sharith," she said. "Not even Markasset was born in Thagorn. Yet you lead

121

them. You have told me how you resisted becoming Captain. You have also told me that you have few regrets for it now, and you have come to believe that the event has some significance to our task."

She half-turned toward me. She was near the lamp, and shadows flickered across her face with the wavering, reflected candleglow. "Six months ago, the idea of serving as High Lord of Eddarta would have appalled me. Three moons ago, I had accepted the idea, but was very frightened. Today—" She turned to face me. Her hands were at her sides, balled into fists. "Today, Rikardon, I found a part of my destiny. I know it. I think if you will let yourself see, you know it too."

It was hard to watch the torment in her face, her eyes.

"You are asking me to abandon the responsibility I *know* is mine," she said.

"I'm not forcing you to choose between Eddarta and Raithskar, Tarani. All I want—what I believe is right—is for you to delay your work in Eddarta until the matter of the Ra'ira is settled for certain."

"I have begun here with a pledge to work for change and betterment, for both Lord and landservant," Tarani said. "To leave now would mean breaking that pledge and destroying the faith and goodwill I can already feel building among the Lords."

I forced back the panic I was feeling, and kept my voice soft as I asked: "Are you saying that you won't go?"

"I am saying that I am not convinced of the *need* for me to go," she answered, "and I am unwilling to risk the damage to my cause in Eddarta on the *chance* that we do not have the true Ra'ira in our safekeeping.

"Rikardon, please try to understand. I am still committed to our original task, but we have no real and recent experience with the Ra'ira, and no reliable way to judge whether this"—she pointed—"is or is not the powerstone.

"Conjecture is not enough, my love."

"If it were real," I said, "it would be easy to prove it. You, Indomel—Zefra, probably—could use it. But proving a negative is nearly impossible, Tarani. You tell me—is there anything that would convince you that this is *not* the Ra'ira?"

She snatched it from my hand and threw it at the floor with a lot of strength.

It bounced.

She kicked it against the wall, knocking a puff of dust from her glith-hide boots.

It ricocheted toward the window and hit the stone sill, narrowly missing a diamond-shaped pane of glass.

I picked it up from where it landed and examined it beside the lamp. It seemed to be undamaged. I handed it back to Tarani.

"Good try," I said. "The fact that it didn't shatter like the duplicate Indomel broke means that it's either the real Ra'ira or a better duplicate."

She tossed the stone lightly, thinking.

"I see your point about negative proof," she said. "Let us leave it at this: one more item of evidence that the stone is powerless will convince me." She tossed the blue gemstone to me. "Until then, I shall continue to work at being High Lord."

"I'm not sure that's fair," I said. I waited long enough for her to tense up, then I smiled. "But I accept it."

I put the Ra'ira—or not—into the small, decorative box and tucked the box under my arm.

"I have only one more question," I said. "Where do I sleep?"

She laughed, and offered me her hand.

17

We were up early the next morning. After we had bathed and dressed (the Ra'ira went with me to the bathhouse), Tarani asked that our breakfast be served in the High Lord's suite.

Indomel and his predecessors had lived very well, and their personal living quarters were roomy and luxurious. Delicate tapestries adorned the walls, and all the furniture was made with fine materials and studied craftsmanship.

"The family's doing fine," I reported, after the servers had left our food on the table in the small dining room. "Keeshah says there is plenty of game, and the cubs are pretty nearly pulling their own weight in the hunting department these days."

"Yayshah seems content, as well," Tarani said. She was tearing a piece of bread into little pieces. I grabbed her hands.

"Ricardo had a relative—his grandmother—who used to tell him: 'Suppose you talk about what's worrying you, boy, instead of taking it out on my good food.'"

Tarani smiled, and turned one hand upward to grab hold of mine and squeeze. She had long, tapered fingers that were, like the rest of her body, stronger than they looked.

"I was thinking that if we had no question as to the authenticity of *this* Ra'ira, you would be leaving soon. When you mentioned the sha'um, I wondered about the cubs. I have been assuming they would remain here, with Yayshah. But their mindlink with you creates as strong a bond as the parental bond to Yayshah."

"If we have to separate," I said, "it will be because I need to take the stone back to Raithskar as quickly as possible. Keeshah can travel faster without the cubs." I squeezed her hand. "And I could be back sooner."

"There must be a decision point," she said. "Do you not feel the urgency?"

"I feel it very strongly. If we have the Ra'ira, it is needed in Raithskar. If we don't have it, then *we* are needed in Raithskar. I understand what you're trying to say, Tarani. You've given me the opportunity to convince you, but the time frame can't be open-ended. You said that a ceremony is planned to install you as High Lord?"

"Day after tomorrow," she said, nodding.

"I wouldn't ask you to leave before that. Shall we agree to start for Raithskar the morning after the Celebration Dance? Whoever is going back?"

She looked relieved.

"Agreed," she said.

"I don't think we'll have to wait all that time before the issue is settled, however," I said, taking a sip of water. "I remembered something while I was bathing this morning that may constitute the evidence we need, if we can find it. If you can spare me today to help me look for it, then *not* finding it will convince *me* that—that I'll need to ride out of Eddarta alone."

"Can you doubt I would help?" she asked. "What is this piece of evidence?"

"When Gharlas first told us about the Ra'ira's power—we were in Dyskornis—he mentioned finding a book, a diary written by one of the Kings. That's how *he* learned about the stone's usefulness. I should think that diary would contain a description of the stone and, perhaps, a description of what it feels like to use it.

"*If* we can find it, and *if* it does describe a subjective experience of using the stone, and *if* that description says that it's one, easy, and two, imparts a kind of power feedback so that one would *know* the stone's power was active—will that convince you that what we have here is Volitar's second replica?"

"It would not speak to the possibility of the mindgift changing across the years," she said, "but yes, I would

125

consider that enough evidence to make my returning to Raithskar to find the truth worth the risk of leaving Eddarta now." She frowned. "You told Indomel of the book, and he searched for it in vain, both in the vault and in Gharlas's home. How do you expect to find it?"

I finished eating, and cleaned my hands on the linen napkin.

"That's where you come in," I said. "Gharlas used the old passage called Troman's Way to get into the vault unseen, right?"

She nodded.

"Troman built that passage so he could visit his paramours in secret. If he had that kind of a mind, why might he not build a secret hiding place inside the house, as well?"

"If he did," Tarani said, "would it not be hidden in the same way as the entrance to Troman's Way, and open only when weight was applied to the floor tiles in a specific pattern?"

"Very likely," I said. "If Gharlas knew one entry code—why would he not know the other?"

She dropped a piece of fruit on her plate and stared at me, growing pale. "You are not proposing that I—that we—enter the All-Mind and search Gharlas's memory?"

Her reaction made me hesitate. "Well, yes," I said, "that's what I was thinking."

She shook her head almost violently. "No. Even if I could bear the thought of touching that mad mind," she said, shuddering, "Recorder training forbids contact with the recently dead." She held up her hand. "I do not know why. I do know that such rules are not given without reason. I cannot do it."

"Troman, then," I pressed her. "*Someone* who knew whether the hiding place is there, and how to open it."

"Troman," she repeated, calming down. "Yes, that is possible." She dropped her napkin on the table. "The food we have eaten will keep our bodies strong while we seek," she said. "I will instruct the household staff that we are not to be disturbed."

A few minutes later, we were lying side by side on the double-thickness pallet that served as a bed. We held

126

hands, and I stared at the ceiling while Tarani breathed deeply, preparing.

I had my own preparation to make, minimizing the Ricardo aspect of my mind to allow this purely Gandalaran force to take hold of me. It occurred to me to wonder if Antonia's memories might interfere with Tarani's action as a Recorder—Tarani had been able to act as Recorder in Kä only because Antonia actively kept out of the way.

I was relieved when Tarani began the formal ritual.

"Will you seek?"

"I will seek, Recorder," I said.

"What do you seek?"

I had to think about that a moment; Somil had taught me that the seeker's goal must be phrased very specifically.

"I want to know whether there is a second secret door in Gharlas's house, and how to open it."

"Then make your mind one with mine, as I have made mine one with the All-Mind. . . ."

The sensation of *separateness* from my body was familiar now, but still disquieting. And my vision of the All-Mind as a huge and roughly spherical, congested network of interconnected rods was no less beautiful than on the other two occasions. Each rod was a cylinder of light, shining and translucent.

. . . *We begin*, said Tarani's mindvoice.

I was only a place, a presence. Seeking with Tarani was a little different from seeking with Somil. I might have noticed the contrast in Kä, except that urgency had driven us to hurry.

Somil's presence had enclosed mine. Tarani's presence touched mine closely, but did not surround it. A physical analogy might be that Somil had carried me, but Tarani and I walked hand in hand. Still, there was no doubt that Tarani was controlling our movement.

Each of the shining bars represented the lifememory of a person, birth to death—not their personalities, but only their memories. A study of Gandalaran history would begin at the center of the sphere and work toward the amorphous glow that marked its outermost edge. Tarani skimmed quickly along the network just inside the boundary of light.

I am searching for Gharlas, she said.

I thought you couldn't share memory with him.

No. But I will know him, and begin our search first with his family.

She pulled us along at a dizzying speed, hovering so that it was her presence, and not mine, that came into contact with the cylinders of light. The sideways rush stopped abruptly. We were "resting" on a cylinder that extended all the way to the edge of the sphere, its far end merging with the glow. Tarani pulled us in the direction of the distant center of the sphere, moving slowly.

She had not gone far when she stopped us and said: *This man was uncle to Gharlas, and lived in the house before him. I touched him only lightly, yet I know he had the secret to Troman's Way.*

He's probably the one who gave it to Gharlas, I said.

Will you share memory with this one, or do you wish only Troman?

Do we have time for both, if we don't find the answer here? I asked.

Yes.

Then I will try this man, I agreed.

I was a young boy, sitting on the patterned floor of the midhall and playing with a set of the dice-like mondeana. One piece skittered away, and I rose on one knee to reach for it.

The tile underneath my knee moved slightly, and I lost interest in the mondeana. I shifted my weight, feeling the tile move. I tested the tiles around that one triangular piece, and found them to be solidly mounted. I tried all the nearby tiles that were the same color of blue, and found three that moved.

I was alone in the house, sulking a little because my older brother was at the second testing, and my father had gone down to the city, to commission a Celebration gift for the next High Lord. He didn't expect my brother, Usal, to be selected as the successor to the present High Lord. Everyone knew there were only two who had a real chance: Horinad, the son of the present High Lord; and Tinis, of the house of Rusal. Today they—and the other fifteen-year-old boys who had shown some outward sign of a mindgift—

128

would know the answer for which they had waited for three years.

The tiles absorbed my attention, and I began a game with them. I jumped with both feet from one to another. They were just large enough for one whole foot and another toe to rest on them comfortably. I straddled the distance between two of the tiles, but they were a little too far apart to make staying like that comfortable.

The four tiles formed a rough square, and I began to imagine lines drawn between them, wondering how many ways they could be connected. I acted out the drawing I imagined by jumping between the tiles. Starting with the tile furthest from the wall, I "connected" the square around the tiles, going first in one direction, then the other. I "drew" crossed lines, starting with the first line toward the wall, then doing it again with the first line parallel to the wall. . . .

The wall moved.

The sound made me jump backward. I stepped on one of the mondeana and it slid out from under me. I landed with a painful jolt on my backside. I hardly noticed the pain, I was so excited. A strip of wall as wide as a man had pulled back and slid aside, revealing a narrow alcove with shelves carved into the back wall. I stared at the alcove, wondering who and how and why. And while I stared, I heard the same faint grating sound, and the wall closed up again.

"No!" I shouted, finally roused from my trance. I ran to the wall, pushed at it, barely pulled my fingers out of the way as the wood-paneled section moved forward to blend in again with the rest of the long wall.

I was crushingly disappointed, until I made the connection: the tiles must be the key. I struggled to remember the patterns I had used, and I recreated them carefully.

The wall opened again, and I shrieked with delight. I grabbed a small table and dragged it to the opening and wedged it there. Once I had made sure that I wasn't going to be trapped inside, I climbed over the table, so excited I could scarcely breathe.

There were only a few things on the shelves: a pretty necklace, a pouch of old coins (the pouch tore as I lifted it, and I raked the coins into a haphazard pile on the lowest

129

shelf), and a small piece of glazed clay. There were markings on the clay, and I climbed back over the table to take the clay into the light.

It seemed to be part of a tile, the same color blue as the ones that moved. There were two separate markings—one a rectangle, and the other a crisscrossed set of lines with numbers marked inside the open areas. The lines reminded me of something. . . .

The pattern of the tiles on the floor!

18

I looked more closely at the rectangle. There was a mark, close to one end, beside an area of the outline marked with a double scoring. I had been excited since finding the secret door; I went positively wild with glee when I figured out the diagram. It was a line sketch of the midhall, only slightly more narrow than it was long. The double scoring occurred on the diagram where there were doors in the room, and the mark inside the outline was beside the widest door—the front door of the house.

I oriented the diagram and ran to a spot to the right of the door. I tested one of the blue tiles. Sure enough, it moved—not enough to be really noticeable if you merely walked across it, but it did move.

Working with the crosshatched diagram, I located the exact tiles that matched the ones with numbers on them. There were twenty in all. I took a deep breath, stepped on the one marked "one" on the diagram, and followed the number sequence.

Another section of the wall slid in and to the side, with very little noise.

I yelled and jumped around the room. The door closed again while I was celebrating, but I was confident I could reopen it. I did, and my skin prickled when I looked inside. The second door opened, not on a closet, but on a stairway that led downward, to the right of the opening. The light from inside the room showed me only about ten steps; the rest was in darkness.

I pulled my head out of the opening when I heard the

door start to close again. Exploring that stairway, I decided with a shiver, was a task for another time. The closet, now—ah, that was a real find.

I ran back over to it and climbed over the table to get inside. I examined the inside wall, and found two shallow, finger-width depressions, positioned vertically, one above the other. They held strips of bronze, mounted with a single pinning so that the short end would rotate into the depression when the longer end was pulled out. They were very close to the opening in the wall; I had to push hard against the door to slide it back from the table a little way. I kept my shoulder pressed against the door while I pulled out the bronze strips, then released the door slowly. Its edge pressed up against the bronze pieces and stopped. I picked up the table and moved it back where I had gotten it, feeling proud for having figured that out.

Now I could move freely in and out of the closet, and I implemented the plan that had occurred to me the moment after I had recovered from the shock of the door opening. I ran to my room and pulled my sketches out from under the stack of folded clothes in the closet.

I wanted to sit down and look through them, but my father was due back at any moment, so I just gathered them and raced back to the closet. I didn't even take time to display them the way I had wanted to, when I saw the shelves. I just set them, still stacked, on one of the higher shelves. I started to close the door, then remembered the marked tile. After I had retrieved it from the far side of the room and put it on a shelf, I pushed on the door, reset the bronze stays into their slots, and stepped out into the midhall. The door slid into position behind the opening, then moved forward until it was flush with the wall.

The moment that door was closed, relief and a feeling of security washed over me. I had lived in fear that my father would find the sketches. There were pitifully few of them now.

My hands tensed into fists as I remembered the day my father had found me beside the city gate, drawing a picture of the vleks pulling the rafts through the river gate. He had dragged me home and beaten me. "How dare you disgrace our family by doing artisan work in public?" he had raged.

He had demanded all my drawings, and had forced me to tear them into shreds and burn them. He had become more gentle then, but I still didn't understand what he had tried to tell me. "You are of the Seven Families, son," he had said, kneeling beside me. "Our family has enough artisans as landservants to produce any image you would like to have. What you were doing is their work, and by doing it yourself, you deprive them of their trade."

He had ended by forbidding me ever to sketch again, and the incident frightened me enough that I had obeyed him, for a time. But there was a force inside me that I simply could not control. Something drove me to begin to sketch again, fearfully, and in secret. I tried to be ashamed, but the pleasure of releasing that force was too great. So I hid the paper and ink and brush, and I checked my closet every day to make sure the sketches had not been discovered.

Only now, I could stop worrying about that. I would continue to keep my supplies in my room. The risk of having them found was worth the convenience of having them available. And I would use the pile of folded trousers as a temporary hiding place. But the bulk of my work, my guilty treasure, was safely hidden.

My head jerked around at the sound of Usal's voice, shouting. The front door slammed open, and he ran in. I stared at him, open-mouthed. He was more dressed up than I had ever seen him. I was seeing him for the first time as a man, not a boy. And he was pale and shaky—more upset than I had ever seen him.

"Where is Father?" he asked me. When I didn't answer right away, he grabbed my shoulders and shook me.

"H-he's in the city," I stammered. "B-back soon." My brother pushed me away and began to pace up and down the room, nearly running. "Usal, what happened?"

"What happened?" he repeated. "Horinad was named High Lord successor."

That sparked my curiosity, in spite of Usal's agitation.

"What about Tinis?" I asked. "Everyone said—you even said—that he would test higher than Horinad."

"He said he did," Usal told me, with a grim tone in his voice that frightened me. "He stood up and told the Lords so, just after they came back into the waiting room and announced Horinad was the one. He said they had changed the test scores, because they were afraid of him. He—he—"

Usal choked up and couldn't go on. I went over to him and touched his arm, alarmed for him, afraid of what he would say, unsure how to comfort him. His other hand whipped around and caught my wrist in a painful grip. I withstood the pain, because of the look in Usal's face. He wasn't seeing me, or the room. He was looking into the waiting room, remembering.

"Some of us . . . laughed at him, but I got scared right away." I nodded, believing and agreeing. Usal knew Tinis very well, and had good reason to respect his power.

"I saw their point," my brother continued. "I mean, Tinis has always been so arrogant, always trying to prove that he's better than anyone else. Some of us were glad to see him beaten. If it had been anyone besides Tinis, I might have laughed too. But I knew Tinis wouldn't leave it there.

"He—he had a sort of fit. Started screaming—I've never seen him so angry. Then he got this peculiar look on his face and just stared at the six Lords, where they were standing in a clump.

"Merthyn was the first," Usal said. His hand still held me, and I could feel him trembling. "Merthyn's eyes went all strange, and he pulled out his dagger and—and—and c-cut his own throat."

Usal swallowed.

"Stop," I whimpered, not knowing whether I meant stop talking or stop hurting my wrist. He didn't hear me.

"Then Hissem," he said. "Then Linel. Three Lords dead in less time than it takes to walk across this room. Blood everywhere, running like rivers around our boots."

He closed his eyes for a moment, and seemed a little calmer when he spoke again.

"Horinad was the only one who understood what was happening. When another Lord drew out his dagger, he yelled 'Tinis, stop it,' and we all jumped on Tinis and started hitting him. He didn't even try to defend himself; he just kept staring in that funny way. We finally knocked him out, but by that time Turenad was dead, too."

"Four Lords? Dead?" I whispered. My brother nodded grimly. "What did they do to Tinis?"

"*Somebody called in the High Guard, and they carried him off. I don't know what they will do, but I know what I hope they'll do.*" His eyes focused, and he finally looked at me again. It was creepy. "*I hope they kill him,*" he said fiercely. "*Because I know him. If they let him live . . .*" He shuddered.

I was pulled away from the boy's memory. I resisted fiercely, struggling to get back to that youthful mind, with its pureness of fear and delight and creativity.

It is time to leave, Tarani's mindvoice told me.

But—yes, Recorder, I said.

We retraced our course, coming back, I somehow knew, to the exact same place where we had entered the All-Mind.

Calm yourself, Tarani urged me, and I tried. The boy's intense feelings had left me in turmoil. They faded gradually until Tarani said: *We shall now return to ourselves*.

The brightness faded.

And I shall withdraw my mind from yours. . . .

A sensation of landing, and sudden coolness.

"Rikardon?" said Tarani's physical voice, sounding weak.

"Yes, I'm here. I'm back," I assured her.

"Good. We should rest for a time."

After we startled the household staff by requesting a midmorning snack twice the size of our breakfast—and ate it all—Tarani and I set out for the house we thought had been Gharlas's. I was faintly surprised that no one wanted to tag along, and I realized that my reaction was colored by Ricardo's conditioning to expect heads of state to have a personal guard with them at all times.

Tarani had shared my experience with the boy's life-memory. She had been about to drag me away after the boy shut the closet door, but she had sensed my curiosity at the entry of the brother, and had allowed me some extra time. I was grateful. Zefra had mentioned that Pylomel had learned not to show his power through an example from his father's generation. Learning of Tinis from the boy had felt like finally scratching an itch I had never really noticed before.

135

We hurried along the cobbled walkway, which wound through garden areas to provide a link between the widely spaced homes. The house Gharlas had lived in was still unoccupied, and we had no trouble getting inside. The condition of the midhall—a tapestry torn, tables overturned—told us that no one had bothered to clean the place up after Gharlas died. The sight called up a chilling memory of the fight that had happened in this room. Tarani, Thymas, and I—we had come very close to death that night.

Tarani shuddered. "I would judge the closet to be about . . . here," she said, and knelt to test the tiles. "Do you remember the sequence?"

"I might," I said, "but if a ten-year-old boy could strike the right combination by accident, we can certainly figure it out by trial and error. I expect this combination is pretty simple. After all, Troman kept the other key written down, so he wouldn't lose it. Would he lock the key away if there were a good chance he'd forget the combination?"

"No, I suppose not. Here," she said, standing up and pointing. "These four."

Those tiles might have been big enough for a boy's feet, but they barely accommodated my toes. After some experimentation, I discovered I could move the tiles by standing with the ball of my foot centered on them, leaning forward slightly.

"I'll try the boy's last pattern first," I said, stepping carefully and feeling a bit awkward.

Nothing happened.

I tried a combination of eight. Then, judging that eight was probably too many, I tried the boy's last five steps, then his last six—and the wall moved.

Tarani was inside the closet almost before the wall stopped moving. It went to the far wall, hesitated, and started sliding forward again. There was just enough time to fish out the bronze stays to keep the door open.

We turned to face the shelves; they looked hugely different from the boy's memory. Gharlas had removed most of the treasure from the High Lord's vault, replacing the items one by one with fakes. The real treasure was here, heaped and piled and stuffed into the shelves.

"If that book exists," I said, "it ought to be here."

Tarani took the bottom of the six shelves, and I took the top one. Most of the items were jewelry, gold or silver settings weighted down with huge gemstones. We couldn't exactly rummage through those stacks; we had to move each item from one pile into another.

The high shelf was less crowded than the others, and it didn't take me long to pile-shift my way from one end of it to the other. When I moved the last item—a filigree gold box—my hand hit something flat that didn't feel like stone.

"I've found something," I said, and Tarani stood up.

I groped, and gathered, and finally brought down a half-inch stack of flat paper in different sizes. I turned the top one over.

It was a sketch of a vlek team, drawing a raft through the river gate. It was a *good* sketch. Tarani took it from my hand and held it to the light.

"How barbaric, that his father should try to stifle this gift," she said. "I shall add this to my list of changes."

She handed the drawing back to me and went back to digging through the bottom shelf. I noticed, on looking carefully, that each shelf had a little stack of paper at one end.

The boy had his own art gallery on display in here, I thought sadly. *Until the "boy"—Gharlas's uncle—passed on, and left his treasure and his secret to his greedy nephew. Gharlas probably just shoved these aside, to start piling up his stolen treasure.*

I couldn't resist looking at the sketches I held. These, from the top shelf, seemed to be the boy's early work and, except for the vlek drawing, they were portraits, some full-body, some faces only. They were remarkably good, never mind that the artist was only ten years old at the time.

The portraits had the subjects' names written on them. Considering the general attitude toward the arts in Lord City, they had to have been drawn from memory, or after long and clandestine study. The boy's father was there, showing a fond sternness that I was sure the boy had softened some.

The last two portraits interested me most, considering

the last event I had shared with the artistic boy. Both were full-body studies, with a believable background of garden pathway. One was Horinad, who had the extreme height that had marked his son, Pylomel, and was softened slightly in his granddaughter. The face showed a striking resemblance to Indomel's, except that it was fuller, and there was a trace of humor around the mouth.

The boy must have done these before the fiasco at the testing, I thought. *Horinad looks about fifteen here; that fits.* I reset Horinad's portrait to the bottom of the stack I held. *Now, let's have a look at the mysterious Tinis.*

"I found it," Tarani said, and stood up. She held a thick sheaf of paper, held together with a strip of leather threaded in and out of small punctures. "Did you hear me, Rikardon? I have the evidence we are seeking—or at least part of it." She touched an edge of the first sheet carefully. "It is fragile, and much too long to read here," she said. "Shall we close the door, and take the book back to our rooms?"

When I didn't reply, she transferred the book into one hand and tugged at my tunic sleeve with the other.

"Rikardon? Were you not eager to find this book?"

"It doesn't matter now," I said. My voice sounded distant to me.

"What? But you wanted evidence—"

"I've found it," I said. "Enough to convince *me*." I handed her the final drawing.

She put the book down and accepted the paper, but she searched my face for a moment before she looked at it, puzzled. "It is Tinis." She shook her head. "Rikardon, I don't understand."

I rubbed my face with my hand, trying to clear my head of the shock I felt.

"Gharlas's uncle was a good artist," I explained. "See, this portrait of Horinad, how much he looks like Pylomel? That tells me that the boy had a gift for accuracy."

"So this portrait of Tinis probably *looks* like Tinis, is that what you are trying to say?"

She was still groping, and I was recovering, so I put it as clearly as possible.

"Tinis is alive," I said. "He lives in Raithskar, under the name of Ferrathyn."

I tapped the sketch.

"I think we found a motive for a Supervisor to want the Ra'ira for himself, don't you?"

19

Tarani was furiously busy for the next two days. We returned from Gharlas's house barely before noon, and she rushed off to Lord Hall for the "educational" meeting with the Lords. That lasted until nearly midnight, and the next day was an endless round of conferences—with each of the Lords, with some of the Harthim landservants. Each family owned all their resources in common, and the distribution of wealth was handled by the Lord. Tarani took an intense course in Lord City politics and economics on the second day.

The morning of the third day was spent in preparation for the ceremony that would install Tarani in her new position and give everybody an excuse for a roaring party. Tarani wished out loud that she had brought the black outfit from Raithskar, but then she found some out-of-style gowns in a closet somewhere. She called me into our suite to help select one for her, and while I was there, the seamstress arrived.

Tarani tried things on, and the seamstress and I offered opinions. Tarani more often sided with the seamstress, but I didn't mind. I was glad enough to be able to spend some time in Tarani's company, regardless of what I was doing. Finally the choice was made—a deep red gown with a full hem and openwork sleeves.

It needed alteration, of course. The seamstress was an older woman with a competent look about her. It was hard for me not to laugh at the look on her face when Tarani sat beside her, picked up a needle and thread, and started work on one side of the hem.

"I do not doubt your skill, Rena," Tarani said. "But I know how little time there is. I can do only simple things, but if my hands can free yours for the more delicate work, I am willing to use them."

"I—uh—thank you, my Lady—uh—Lord—uh—High Lord—"

Tarani dropped her work and stared at the woman. "Rena, you remind me of a problem. Being addressed by my title—which I do not have officially yet, by the way—feels rather awkward to me, especially when two women are sewing on the same dress. It is a problem that may occur often. Would you be comfortable calling me by my given name?"

"You mean—uh—no, ma'am, it would not be proper."

"A title is necessary?" Tarani asked, musing, and only slightly poking fun at the competent old lady. "Then, will 'Lord Tarani' do?"

A smile lit the lined old face. "Yes, that sounds right, ma'am. Lord Tarani." She tried it out.

"You don't need me any more, do you?" I asked.

Tarani looked up at me and smiled. "Always, my love, but not for this particular task."

I headed for the door, stopping to press my hand against the back of her neck. She arched her back, returning the pressure.

I spent the rest of the morning walking around the Harthim enclosure, becoming familiar with its layout. I wandered into the barracks area, where I was greeted with a mixture of surprise, welcome, and suspicion. One of the welcomes came from a man I regarded as an old friend—Naddam, the man who had been in charge of the Lingis mine before I had been "impressed" as his replacement.

Naddam was drinking faen when I walked into the common room at one end of the barracks, and he choked and sputtered when he saw me. I clapped him on the back, laughing.

"May the fleas bite Harthim where it hurts!" he swore. "You can't be the new High Lord's 'companion,' can you?" He did not wait for me to answer; he had already put two and two together. "Well," he said. "Well, that must be some kind of a record, friend—Lakad?"

"Rikardon," I said.

"Rikardon, then," he repeated laughing. "From the copper mines to Lord Hall in less than four moons. A record, I'd bet on it."

The other guards watched us warily, and I invited Naddam to walk with me a while. I told him what had happened after he left the Lingis mine. He was not happy to learn about the slave escape system that had been run from his mining camp, without his knowledge. He was glad to learn about Tarani's plans for reform in the mines, to reduce the work level to provide punishment, but not exhaustion.

He had heard about our arrival on sha'um, and who I really was, and he was curious why Keeshah had not been around at the mine. I told him about the sha'um and the Sharith, the mating cycle that had deprived me of Keeshah's company, and the special bonding that had brought his mate out of the Valley. He was intrigued, and touched, I thought, by the story.

"I have a favor to ask, Naddam," I said.

"Ask it," he said.

"No one else in Eddarta knows this yet, but Tarani and I are going to have to leave Eddarta again."

"Soon?"

"Tomorrow," I said. "Tarani is making her own preparations, leaving instructions, coordinating projects, that sort of thing. I expect she is setting up some kind of method of communication.

"But all those are *her* preparations. I have faith in her judgment; I would trust anyone she chooses to trust. But I'll feel better if there is one person I, personally, can rely on to keep us informed of what's going on here, while we're in Raithskar."

"So—what do you want me to do?"

"I want you to find a maufel who has been to Raithskar," I said. The bird-handlers could not guide or direct a message bird to a place they had never seen. "There has to be one. And I'll find one in Raithskar who knows Eddarta. All of this is 'just in case,' you understand. I'll be more comfortable knowing that if some emergency does occur, I'll have a fast, direct way to find out about it."

He squinted at me. "But you're not expecting an emergency?"

I laughed. "No, not at all. *Really*," I added, fending off the skepticism that was so evident in his stance.

"Well, whether you are or you aren't," he said, "of course I'll do it."

"Thanks," I said.

All the fuss over the gown had been in aid of finding something to wear to the *party*. For the ceremony, which the Lords called a "naming," Tarani was well prepared. The white tunic with its embroidered emblem—a little more ornate than the embroidery on the tunics of the other Lords—had been fitted to her on our first day in Eddarta.

All the Lord families gathered on one side of the doughnut-shaped hall, crowding together to get a clear view of the portable platform which had been set up across the entryway to the Council Chamber. All the Lords stood on the platform, with Tarani standing regally tall at the center of the row.

Hollin stepped forward and gave a speech about the duties of the High Lord, and each of the other Lords spoke a ritual testimony of respect and group spirit. Their litany did not, I noticed, include a promise of obedience. In theory at least, Lord City itself was an autocracy, run by a specific group of people.

Tarani had a set piece to say, and she delivered it with solemn sincerity. She gave a short speech—mostly gratitude for acceptance of a stranger, and a wish for tolerance of her learning period. She did not mention our plans to leave the next day.

The ceremony was short and the Lords were replaced on the platform by the musicians. The party started.

The next morning—not too early—Tarani dressed in desert tunic and trousers, and it felt like I could release a breath I had been holding for three days. Our travel packs were in our suite, and Tarani packed some extra clothes into hers.

143

She picked up the drawing of Tinis and studied it for a moment.

"I know I have never seen this man," she said. "I mean, of course, an adult version of this boy."

"You haven't," I said. "I saw him while you were in Raithskar, but always while you weren't available to meet him."

"Let us assume that Tinis—or Ferrathyn, I should say—has the true Ra'ira, and sole access to its power. Why would he terrorize Raithskar with uncontrolled vineh?"

"That may be just a side issue," I said. "After all, he is only one man, and has to rest sometimes. It's just not possible for one man to control . . . all . . . those . . ."

I had been reclining on the pallet. I propped myself on my elbow.

"What are you thinking?" Tarani asked me.

"I'm thinking about vineh," I said grimly. "About animals that suddenly acquired a talent for complex strategy." I slammed my open hand on the floor beside the pallet. "I saw it, but I didn't!" I growled. "Remember the vineh that went after the cubs, in the fight? They killed one cub, but they weren't hurting the other two—*because Ferrathyn told them not to*.

"That talk of vineh acquiring some Gandalaran characteristics through long contact with more intelligent minds works logically, up to a point. I can believe that vineh could plan an ambush, or that they could analyze an opponent and attack at the weakest point. But what they did with the cubs was *not* possible for animals. They might have attacked and killed the cubs, because they were weak enemies—comparatively, that is.

"The vineh *used* those cubs to destroy the effectiveness of the other enemies, and that requires an intuitive jump: 'I care for my young, and if they are endangered, it is a distraction from everything else; therefore threatening the young sha'um will disturb the adult sha'um.' *That* is not learned behavior, it is rational thought, and I cannot believe a vineh's mind could have come up with the idea—on its own.

"To answer your question, I believe Ferrathyn has simply let the vineh run free—except when he has a job for them.

144

Even then, he may control only a select few, the natural leaders."

Tarani had listened in silence.

"Then it is Ferrathyn we owe for the death of the lost one," she said quietly. She folded the portrait of Tinis and placed it in her travel bag.

A knock sounded at the door, and Tarani straightened up and crossed the bedroom. At the parlor door, she turned back to me.

"I sent for some people," she said. "This is how I choose to prepare Eddarta for my absence. Please do not interfere."

She crossed the parlor to the hallway door, and I came out from the bedroom, closing the door behind me.

"We are here, as you requested, High Lord," said Hollin when Tarani had opened the door. She stepped back and Hollin, Zefra, and Indomel came into the room.

It's a good thing she warned me to stay out of this, I thought, settling into a chair in a corner. *I wouldn't have Zefra and Indomel in the same room, ever again.*

Each of the people registered surprise when they saw the way Tarani was dressed. She had taken care to stand out of the sight of anyone else in the hall, and now she closed the door.

Hollin I would describe as "solid." He had size, and weight, and middle-aged good looks, and slow mannerisms that gave him an air of steadiness. The few times I had been within earshot of him, he had been giving clear directions or well-considered opinions, and he impressed me as already being committed to support of Tarani.

He looked uncomfortable in the presence of Indomel.

"Thank you for coming," Tarani said. "You have guessed that I depart today on a journey. You three are the only ones who are to know where I have gone, and why. Hollin, I know this will put you in a difficult position among the Lords, but I require your consent to secrecy."

"You have it, gladly," he said. "It must be a matter of extreme importance."

It's a damn good thing she warned me to stay out of it, I thought, as I watched Tarani open the small box and take out the Ra'ira.

She told them the whole story. The only thing she held back was the fact that she and I were both human-Gandalaran blends. She covered that in her description of our encounter with Gharlas, saying only that we had discovered that we had a kind of natural immunity to compulsion.

She told them about Tinis too—now known as Ferrathyn.

"I *am* convinced," she said, with the faintest possible smile flashed in my direction, "that Tinis has the real stone. He also has command of hundreds of vineh, possibly with the capability to control an army of people. From what we learned of him in the All-Mind, he has a great capacity for anger. Would anyone doubt that his anger is aimed at Eddarta?"

Three people shook their heads. Hollin was pale.

"Regaining control of the true Ra'ira has become more than merely a task to which Rikardon and I are committed, to which we feel destined. It has become an imperative defensive measure for Eddarta, to which I am newly committed, and to which I feel destined.

"I *must* leave today for Raithskar, and I cannot say when I shall return."

Nobody had bothered to sit down. The three of them woke from the near-trance induced by Tarani's story. It was Indomel who broke the silence.

"High Lord," he said, with a tone of contempt carefully calculated to be tolerable, "I understand why you have chosen to tell Hollin all this. He is an able administrator, and would have been my choice for so sensitive a matter."

Well, live and learn, I thought. *The kid does have some good sense.*

"And Zefra," Indomel continued, "is your mother, and it is fitting that you share confidences with her. But I—I, sister, am your opponent and your enemy. Why am I here this morning?"

"You and Zefra," Tarani said coolly, "are here for identical reasons. Hollin will have all he can do to keep the Lords working toward the goals we have outlined, without having to be concerned about the two of you. You are ambitious, each of you—for different purposes, in different directions, yet you are alike in this."

146

Zefra sputtered with outrage; Indomel smiled.

"One, I wanted you both to know that this"—she tossed the stone—"is worthless, so you will not kill each other trying to get it, after I leave."

This time, Indomel laughed out loud. Zefra crossed her arms tightly against her chest and snapped her mouth shut. Tarani was not blind to her agitation.

"I would do this more gently, Mother, if I had the time; I have already explained that there is too little time as it is.

"You two," she said to them, "are the key to the Lords working well with Hollin. I know that you each have established contacts, owed favors, and the like, within the families. If you wanted to undermine my position during my absence, it would be easy for you.

"I want you to *confirm* my position," she said. "Squelch rumors of abandonment, encourage belief that I will be back, that my commitment to Eddarta continues. If you work your contacts in my favor, Hollin's job will be much easier."

"Why would we do that?" Indomel asked. "Why, in particular, would *I* do that?"

"Because it is the price of your remaining in Eddarta," Tarani said. "You must agree to two conditions, or I will leave orders for your transport to the Lingis mine."

I think everybody except Tarani gasped.

"You will be given no duty," she said, "but you will be kept isolated, with a special guard of six men—more, I hope, than even both of you could control through compulsion at one time." She smiled. "You will be in comfortable quarters, I shall see to that. But you *will* be living in the same quarters."

After contemplating the Lingis vision for a few seconds, Indomel growled: "What are your terms?"

"First, that you use whatever influence you have only to support me and the programs I have initiated."

Zefra spoke up first. "Agreed, daughter," she said sweetly, all trace of her agitation vanished. "I would have done so in any case."

"Indomel?"

The boy walked away from the others, turned back, shrugged. "Agreed," he said. "The second term?"

"You must each give me your promise that you will not use your mindgifts *in any way* during my absence."

Zefra flinched, and Indomel laughed.

"Ah, that hurts, does it not, Mother? A vow to support your daughter does not restrict you from trying to destroy your son—is that why the first condition pleased you so?"

"Indomel," Tarani snapped, "do you agree to the second term?"

The boy straightened his face. "Yes, I agree," he said. "And I am as little happy with it as Zefra."

"Mother?"

Zefra glared at her son for a moment, then sighed and relaxed. "Agreed."

"Hollin, I hold you witness to their acceptance of those terms, and appoint you as the sole judge of their compliance or violation. You are empowered to implement the Lingis arrangement at any time you deem it necessary."

Hollin only nodded, looking a little awed.

"Meanwhile, remove the guards from their rooms. They shall live in this house as part of my family, not as my prisoners, as long as they meet the stated terms."

"All understood, High Lord," Hollin said.

She sighed heavily.

"Then all is done, and I may go. Goodbye."

She hugged her mother, touched Hollin's shoulder, but offered Indomel no gesture. He looked surprised, and then he smiled. "I begin to believe, sister, that your tenure as High Lord will be an interesting time."

END PROCEEDINGS:
INPUT SESSION SIX

—*I withdraw our minds from the All-Mind, and now mine from yours. . . .*

—*Your body is tense. What troubles you?*

—*Anger, Recorder. I had only begun to see the deceit and misdirection Ferrathyn had applied, with regard to the "missing" Ra'ira. And I had not yet accepted that the kindly old man who had inspired my trust had ruthlessly manipulated and endangered an entire city.*

—*Be calm. Rest. Your anger will find expression during the next session.*

—*Recorder?*

—*Yes.*

—*Thank you, again, for reminding me of the importance of the Record.*

—*You are welcome. Now sleep.*

ABOUT THE AUTHORS

RANDALL GARRETT and VICKI ANN HEYDRON met in 1975 in the California home of their mutual agent, Tracy E. Blackstone. Within a year, they had decided to begin working together and, in December 1978, they were married.

Currently, they are living in Austin, Texas, where they are working on the Gandalara novels, of which *The Steel of Raithskar* is the first, *The Glass of Dyskornis* second, *The Bronze of Eddarta* third, *The Well of Darkness* fourth, *The Search for Kä* fifth, and *Return to Eddarta* sixth.

The sixth volume in a stirring science fiction series

RETURN TO EDDARTA

by Randall Garrett & Vicki Heydron

Their mission to the fabled lost city of Kä a resounding success, Rikardon and Tarani begin the long trek back to Eddarta, seat of the government of Eddarta. There, they discover shocking treachery—and Tarani must call on all her strength to reclaim her rightful place on Eddarta's throne.

Don't miss any of the exciting titles in **THE GANDALARA CYCLE:**

"The series as a whole is possibly the best of its kind in many years."
—*S.F. Chronicle*

All the books in **THE GANDALARA CYCLE** are available wherever Bantam Books are sold, or use this handy coupon for ordering:

Bantam Books, Inc., Dept. SF 26, 414 East Golf Road,
Des Plaines, Ill. 60016

Please send me the books I have checked above. I am enclosing $_____
(please add $1.25 to cover postage and handling: send check or money order—no cash or C.O.D.'s please).

Mr/Ms _____

Address _____

City/State _____ Zip _____

SF 26—2/85

Please allow four to six weeks for delivery. This offer expires 9/85.
Prices and availability subject to change without notice.

Coming in 1985 . . .

The climax of the Gandalara Cycle:

THE
RIVER
WALL

by Randall Garrett and Vicki Ann Heydron

The seventh and final volume in the tale of Ricardo Carillo, a man swept from his own time and place to an exotic world in the midst of a titanic power struggle. In *The River Wall*, he at last discovers the real location of Gandalara—and his true role in the clash between its rulers. A triumphant conclusion to the series the *Science Fiction Chronicle* called "possibly the best of its kind in many years."

SPECIAL MONEY SAVING OFFER

Now you can have an up-to-date listing of Bantam's hundreds of titles plus take advantage of our unique and exciting bonus book offer. A special offer which gives you the opportunity to purchase a Bantam book for only 50¢. Here's how!

By ordering any five books at the regular price per order, you can also choose any other single book listed (up to a $4.95 value) for just 50¢. Some restrictions do apply, but for further details why not send for Bantam's listing of titles today!

Just send us your name and address plus 50¢ to defray the postage and handling costs.

OUT OF THIS WORLD!

That's the only way to describe Bantam's great series of science fiction classics. These space-age thrillers are filled with terror, fancy and adventure and written by America's most renowned writers of science fiction. Welcome to outer space and have a good trip!

☐	24709	**RETURN TO EDDARTA** by Garrette & Heydron	$2.75
☐	22647	**HOMEWORLD** by Harry Harrison	$2.50
☐	22759	**STAINLESS STEEL RAT FOR PRESIDENT** by Harry Harrison	$2.75
☐	22796	**STAINLESS STEEL RAT WANTS YOU** by Harry Harrison	$2.50
☐	20780	**STARWORLD** by Harry Harrison	$2.50
☐	20774	**WHEELWORLD** by Harry Harrison	$2.50
☐	24176	**THE ALIEN DEBT** by F. M. Busby	$2.75
☐	24710	**A STORM UPON ULSTER** by Kenneth C. Flint	$3.50
☐	24175	**THE RIDERS OF THE SIDHE** by Kenneth C. Flint	$2.95
☐	23992	**THE PRACTICE EFFECT** by David Brin	$2.75
☐	23589	**TOWER OF GLASS** by Robert Silverberg	$2.95
☐	23495	**STARTIDE RISING** by David Brin	$3.50
☐	24564	**SUNDIVER** by David Brin	$2.75
☐	23512	**THE COMPASS ROSE** by Ursula LeGuin	$2.95
☐	23541	**WIND'S 12 QUARTERS** by Ursula LeGuin	$2.95
☐	22855	**CINNABAR** by Edward Bryant	$2.50
☐	22938	**THE WINDHOVER TAPES: FLEXING THE WARP** by Warren Norwood	$2.75
☐	23351	**THE WINDHOVER TAPES: FIZE OF THE GABRIEL RATCHETS** by Warren Norwood	$2.95
☐	23394	**THE WINDHOVER TAPES: AN IMAGE OF VOICES** by Warren Norwood	$2.75
☐	22968	**THE MARTIAN CHRONICLES** by Ray Bradbury	$2.75
☐	24168	**PLANET OF JUDGMENT** by Joe Halderman	$2.95
☐	23756	**STAR TREK: THE NEW VOYAGES 2** by Culbreath & Marshak	$2.95

Prices and availability subject to change without notice.

Buy them at your local bookstore or use this handy coupon for ordering:

Bantam Books, Inc., Dept. SF, 414 East Golf Road, Des Plaines, Ill. 60016

Please send me the books I have checked above. I am enclosing $_____ (please add $1.25 to cover postage and handling). Send check or money order —no cash or C.O.D.'s please.

Mr/Mrs/Miss _____

Address_____

City_____ State/Zip_____

SF—3/85

Please allow four to six weeks for delivery. This offer expires 9/85.